IT ALWAYS STARTS WITH US

THE GIRL WHO TOUCHED THE SKY

NIKHIL. S

 Scribe

It Always Starts With Us

Copyright © 2025 Nikhil. S

Publisher: Inkscribe Media Pvt. Ltd

ISBN Number: 978-1-966421-64-1

Contents

1. First Impressions 5

2. Late Night Conversation 11

3. Building Trust and Intimacy.................................. 14

4. The Proposal.. 21

5. Charvis Decision.. 27

6. First InPerson Meeting 33

7. Sweet Moments and Adventures 40

8. Nikhils Surprise Visit.. 47

9. Facing Parental Challenges 55

10. Navigating Family Conflicts.................................. 62

11. Compromise and Understanding........................... 69

12. Building Bridges with Family 75

13. Strengthening Their Bond..................................... 81

14. Supporting Each Others Dreams 88

15. Facing External Pressures..................................... 95

16. Planning the Wedding... 101

17. Family Dynamics Shift 107

18. PreWedding Jitters 114

Contents

19. Friends and Celebrations 120

20. The Wedding Eve 126

21. The Wedding Day 132

22. Married Life Begins 138

23. Challenges and Growth 145

24. Celebrating Milestones 151

25. Looking to the Future 158

Acknowledgments *164*

First Impressions 🖤

The notification pinged on Charvi's phone, a tiny vibration that felt oddly significant. She glanced down, her brow furrowing slightly at the unfamiliar username. "Nikhil_lensman," it read, followed by a comment on her latest photo – a sun-drenched shot of a bustling street market, vibrant with color and life. It wasn't a gushing compliment, not a cheesy pick-up line, just a simple observation: "Love the composition; the way you captured the light is amazing."

Charvi smiled, a small, shy smile that softened her features. It wasn't often she received comments from strangers, especially ones that felt so genuine. She scrolled through Nikhil's profile, her fingers lingering on each image. His

photos were just as captivating as hers – street scenes, candid portraits, moments of everyday life captured with a keen eye for detail and a poetic sense of light and shadow. A shared passion, a silent understanding seemed to connect them even before they'd exchanged a single direct message.

Responding felt both exciting and terrifying. The world of online interactions, for Charvi, was a delicate dance between vulnerability and guardedness. She carefully crafted her reply, her fingers hovering over the keyboard, each word chosen with deliberation. "Thank you! Your work is incredible too – I especially love the series on abandoned buildings," she typed, adding a simple heart emoji at the end. It was a small gesture, almost insignificant, but it felt like a bridge thrown across a chasm, a tentative step towards connection.

Nikhil's response was almost instantaneous. "Thanks! Glad you appreciate them. I'm always drawn to the stories hidden in places people overlook." His message was casual, friendly, yet there was an underlying warmth, an unspoken invitation for further conversation.

Their initial exchange was tentative, a careful exploration of common ground. They talked about their favorite photographers, their inspirations, their anxieties about pursuing photography as a career. The conversations flowed effortlessly, each message building on the last, a steady rhythm of shared interests and mutual respect. They discovered a common love for old film cameras, for the tangible feel of developing photos in a darkroom. They even debated the merits of different types of film stock, their digital conversation buzzing with a shared passion that transcended the limitations of the screen.

Days turned into weeks, and their online conversations evolved. They moved beyond photography, exploring other aspects of their lives. Charvi shared her love of classic literature, her anxieties about university applications, her dreams of travelling the world. Nikhil, in turn, revealed his passion for cooking, his close-knit family, and his occasional struggles with self-doubt. The initial cautiousness melted away, replaced by a growing comfort and intimacy. The late- night conversations, filled with laughter and vulnerability, became a highlight of their days, a sanctuary from the often- chaotic realities of their lives.

The virtual world became their shared space, a canvas on which they painted their nascent connection. They discovered online games they both enjoyed, their digital avatars embarking on virtual adventures together. They shared playlists, exchanged song lyrics that resonated with their feelings, built a digital scrapbook of memories, both real and imagined. The internet, often seen as a realm of superficial connections and fleeting interactions, became for them a haven of authenticity and genuine connection. It was a space where they felt seen, understood, and valued for who they were, imperfections and all.

Their late-night conversations, far from being superficial exchanges, delved into the deepest recesses of their hearts. They shared their fears, their insecurities, their dreams – the things they often hesitated to reveal to friends or family. It was in these unguarded moments, in the quiet intimacy of their digital exchanges, that a profound bond began to form. It was a bond built not on fleeting impressions or superficial charm, but on shared vulnerabilities, mutual understanding, and a profound sense of empathy.

One evening, while discussing their anxieties about the future, Nikhil confessed his fear of failure, his uncertainty about his chosen career path. Charvi, listening intently, shared her own fears – her anxieties about living up to her parents' expectations, her apprehension about leaving home for university. In sharing their vulnerabilities, they found solace and strength in each other's words, a comforting reassurance that they weren't alone in their struggles. It was a testament to the trust and intimacy they had cultivated, a silent acknowledgment of the deep connection that was slowly but surely taking root.

Their virtual dates were as imaginative as they were intimate. They'd embark on virtual museum tours, exploring famous art pieces together, their comments and observations enriching the experience. They'd watch movies simultaneously, pausing to discuss scenes and characters, their shared responses forging a sense of connection. They'd even have virtual coffee dates, each preparing their own beverage while chatting via video call, the mundane act made special by their shared presence. These virtual experiences, far from being substitutes for real-world interactions, added a unique dimension to their relationship, building a sense of shared intimacy that extended beyond the limitations of physical space.

The weeks melted into months, and their online interactions became an integral part of their daily routines. Their digital connection was more than just a casual friendship; it was a foundation, a framework upon which a profound emotional bond was built. It was a bond that defied geographical boundaries, a testament to the power of human connection in an increasingly digital world. It was a bond that was slowly, yet surely, leading them towards a future neither could have ever imagined. The stage was set, the foundation was strong, and the next act of their story was about to begin.

Late Night
Conversations 💜

The glow of Charvi's laptop screen illuminated her face, casting long shadows across her bedroom walls. It was late, well past midnight, but sleep was a distant thought. Her fingers danced across the keyboard, composing a message to Nikhil, a response to his latest anecdote – a humorous tale about a disastrous attempt at baking a cake. Laughter bubbled up inside her, a warm feeling that spread through her chest. These late-night conversations were becoming a ritual, a cherished part of her day, a sanctuary where she could be herself, vulnerabilities and all.

Nikhil, on the other side of the screen, was equally engrossed. His room, much like Charvi's, was bathed in the soft glow of his computer monitor. The city lights outside cast a faint luminescence through his window, a silent witness to the unfolding intimacy of their digital exchange. He was meticulously crafting his reply, choosing his words carefully, wanting to capture the nuances of his feelings, the depth of his connection with Charvi.

Their conversations were no longer confined to photography. They ranged from the mundane to the profound, a kaleidoscope of experiences and emotions. They discussed their favorite books, dissecting plot lines and analyzing characters with the passion of seasoned literary critics. They shared their favorite songs, their lyrics weaving a tapestry of shared sentiments, unspoken desires, and quiet yearnings.

They talked about their families, their histories, their dreams, their fears, their hopes for the future – intimate details that revealed the essence of their souls.

One night, Charvi confessed her anxieties about university applications, the pressure to choose the right path, the fear of making the wrong decision. Nikhil listened patiently, his responses thoughtful and empathetic. He shared his own struggles, his doubts about his chosen career, his fear of failure, his insecurities. His words weren't platitudes or empty reassurances; they were honest reflections of his own vulnerabilities, a testament to the trust he placed in Charvi.

In sharing their deepest fears and insecurities, they discovered a strength they hadn't known they possessed. They found solace in each other's words, a comforting reassurance that they weren't alone in their struggles, that their anxieties were shared experiences, and that their imperfections were part of what made them unique and lovable. The late-night conversations were a crucible, forging a bond of trust and understanding that transcended the digital divide.

These conversations, held in the quiet solitude of their respective bedrooms, miles apart yet deeply connected, laid the groundwork for a love story that would defy geographical boundaries, a testament to the power of genuine connection in the digital age. It was a foundation built not on fleeting impressions or superficial charm, but on shared vulnerabilities, mutual understanding, a profound sense of empathy, and the comforting warmth of late-night conversations. The stage was set, and the story was only just beginning.

Building Trust and

Intimacy 🖤

Their online relationship, initially fueled by shared photographs and witty banter, began to evolve. It wasn't just late-night chats anymore; it was the slow, deliberate crafting of a digital connection that felt surprisingly tangible. Nikhil, a whiz at coding, created a shared online space – a virtual haven that was only accessible to them. It was a simple webpage, really, but within its digital confines, they created a world of their own. They uploaded their favorite songs, building a collaborative playlist that morphed into a soundtrack for their budding romance. Each song selection carried unspoken messages, a subtle communication that transcended the limitations of text. A melancholic ballad reflected a shared sadness, a bouncy pop tune represented a moment of shared laughter. The playlist became a living, breathing representation of their evolving emotional landscape.

Their virtual haven extended beyond music. They started playing online games together, their laughter echoing through their headsets as they navigated pixelated worlds and overcame virtual challenges. These weren't just games; they were shared experiences, a testament to their growing comfort and trust. The playful competitiveness fostered a healthy dynamic, adding a layer of lightheartedness to their already deep connection. A particularly memorable evening involved a grueling strategy game that lasted until the early hours of the morning. They argued, strategized, and celebrated their small victories together, creating memories that were as vibrant and real as any shared physical experience.

Beyond the playful escapades of online games, their virtual dates often involved "exploring" the world together. They'd embark on virtual museum tours, meticulously studying paintings and sculptures, sharing their interpretations and opinions with the depth and passion of seasoned art critics. One particularly memorable "date" involved a virtual visit to the Louvre Museum. They spent hours poring over masterpieces, discussing artistic techniques and the historical context of the paintings, their conversation seamlessly flowing from art history to personal anecdotes, building a bridge between intellectual curiosity and emotional intimacy. These virtual excursions were more than just sightseeing; they were a way to deepen their understanding of each other's tastes, passions, and perspectives.

Their virtual world wasn't just a playful escape; it was a safe space where they could explore their vulnerabilities without fear of judgment. They shared personal anecdotes, dreams, and fears, the weight of their words softened by the distance, yet the sincerity palpable through the screen. Nikhil confessed his anxieties about his upcoming final exams, his voice trembling slightly through the headset. Charvi, in response, shared her own struggles with self-doubt and the pressure to live up to the expectations of her family. Their shared vulnerabilities fostered a deeper level of empathy and understanding, solidifying the foundation of their bond.

Their virtual space became a repository of shared vulnerabilities, a testament to the growing trust that flourished between them.

The transition from shy, carefully worded messages to candid, emotionally vulnerable conversations was gradual but profound. It was a testament to the slow, organic nature of their budding relationship. As their comfort levels increased, so did the intimacy of their conversations. They talked about their families, their hopes, their dreams, their fears—the things that shaped their identities and informed their perspectives. They discussed their past relationships, their heartaches, and their lessons learned, revealing a level of vulnerability that is seldom shared during the initial stages of any relationship, physical or otherwise. These candid conversations, free of the pressure of physical proximity, allowed them to connect on a deeper, more intimate level.

Their discussions evolved beyond mere words. They shared playlists, not just of their favorite songs, but of songs that resonated with specific moments in their shared digital journey. They created digital photo albums, sharing images from their lives, capturing fleeting moments that revealed a glimpse into their unique realities. These shared digital spaces became a repository of their shared experiences, forming a tangible record of their evolving connection.

These weren't just files stored on a server; they were the bricks and mortar of their digital relationship, a testament to the growing intimacy and trust that blossomed between them.

One evening, Nikhil surprised Charvi with a virtual scavenger hunt. He crafted a series of clues, each leading to a different piece of their shared digital history. The clues were hidden within their collaborative playlists, their virtual photo albums, even within their online game histories. The hunt itself was a playful adventure, but the underlying message was clear: their relationship was built on shared memories and a growing collection of meaningful moments. The hunt ended with a virtual gift – a digitally rendered version of his favorite photograph, a testament to their shared passion for photography and the depth of their emotional connection.

This virtual world, though separate from their physical realities, became a significant part of their lives. It wasn't a substitute for a physical relationship, but a crucial element in building a solid foundation of trust and intimacy. It was a safe space where they could be themselves, unburdened by the pressures of physical presence and societal expectations. It was a space where their connection could flourish, unhindered by the anxieties and complexities of face-to-face interactions.

As their virtual relationship deepened, their interactions started influencing their physical worlds in subtle ways. Charvi found herself unconsciously incorporating Nikhil's favorite colors into her clothing choices. Nikhil started listening to a genre of music he wouldn't have previously explored, inspired by Charvi's eclectic musical tastes. These small, almost subconscious shifts in their behaviors reflected the growing influence their digital relationship had on their offline lives, blurring the lines between the virtual and the real. The digital world had become a catalyst, accelerating their emotional connection and subtly shaping their individual identities.

Their online conversations were infused with a sense of playfulness that kept their connection light and enjoyable. They'd share silly memes, engage in playful banter, and tease each other, all contributing to a vibrant and engaging dynamic. This lightheartedness served as a counterpoint to the more serious and vulnerable moments, ensuring their interactions remained balanced and fulfilling. This constant interplay between lightheartedness and emotional depth was a key ingredient in building a strong and enduring bond. It prevented the heavier conversations from becoming overwhelming, providing a necessary respite from the intense vulnerability that often accompanied their shared experiences.

One night, sharing a virtual cup of coffee, as represented by a shared animated GIF, Charvi confessed a deep-seated fear about commitment. It wasn't a fear of Nikhil specifically, but rather a fear stemming from past experiences. Nikhil listened patiently, his virtual presence radiating empathy and understanding. He didn't rush her, didn't pressure her; he simply acknowledged her feelings, validating her anxieties and offering reassurance. His response wasn't a grand gesture, but a quiet, heartfelt demonstration of his unwavering support and respect. It was in this moment, in the shared quietude of their virtual space, that their connection truly deepened. It was a testament to the power of empathy, trust, and the quiet strength of a genuine connection built over shared vulnerabilities and countless late-night conversations. Their relationship, born from an Instagram connection, was steadily and surely evolving into something truly extraordinary, a love story that was both modern and timeless, forged in the crucible of shared experiences and a burgeoning, profoundly intimate digital connection. The foundation had been laid, strong and unwavering, ready for whatever the future held.

The Proposal 💕

The notification pinged on Charvi's phone, a small vibration that seemed to carry the weight of the world. It was an Instagram message from Nikhil. She hesitated, a familiar knot tightening in her stomach. It had been months since their initial Instagram connection, months of late-night virtual dates, shared playlists, and whispered secrets across the digital divide. Months of building something extraordinary, something that felt both profoundly real and impossibly fragile.

She clicked on the message, her breath catching in her throat as a video began to play. It wasn't just any video; it was Nikhil, bathed in the soft glow of what looked like his apartment's living room. He looked... different. More mature, somehow. His usual playful grin was replaced with a nervousness that tugged at her heartstrings.

"Charvi," he began, his voice a low, hesitant murmur

against the backdrop of soft, familiar music – their song, the one they'd first shared on their virtual haven, a melancholic ballad that had somehow mirrored their own shared vulnerabilities. "This isn't easy, and I'm probably going to sound like a total mess, but…" He paused, taking a deep breath, the camera slightly shaking in his unsteady hands. "I've been thinking a lot lately… about us, about how far we've come, about the incredible connection we share."

He continued, his words carefully chosen, each syllable imbued with emotion. He spoke of their late-night conversations that stretched into the early hours of the morning, their virtual museum tours, their shared victories in their pixelated online worlds. He reminisced about the painstakingly crafted scavenger hunt, the digital gift, the countless hours they spent building a world together, a world that existed only within the confines of their screens yet felt more real than anything she'd ever known.

He described how their virtual connection had seamlessly bled into their physical lives, how his world had been subtly, yet significantly, altered by her presence, despite the distance. He talked about the way her laughter still echoed in his ears, even when they weren't directly connected; the way her quirky sense of humor still brightened his day, even after the virtual connections ended. He painted a vivid picture of their shared history, their evolution from shy, carefully worded messages to intimate, emotionally vulnerable conversations. He spoke of her strength, her resilience, her unwavering kindness – qualities that had captivated him from the very start.

And then, he said the words that sent shivers down her spine, words that simultaneously thrilled and terrified her. He spoke of his love for her, a love that had blossomed not in the crowded streets of the city, not in a grand, romantic gesture, but within the intimacy of their carefully constructed virtual space. It was a love born of late-night chats, shared vulnerabilities, and a mutual understanding that transcended the limitations of physical proximity.

He pulled a small, velvet box from his pocket, the camera's focus shifting to the tiny object. Inside, nestled on a bed of soft satin, was a ring. Not a diamond, not extravagant or showy, but simple and elegant, reflecting Nikhil's understated charm. A ring, he explained, that represented their unique and extraordinary connection – a ring that was the culmination of countless virtual dates, countless shared memories, and the promise of a future that felt both exciting and utterly terrifying.

"Charvi," he said, his voice choked with emotion, "Will you marry me?"

The video ended. Charvi sat there, stunned, the tiny screen of her phone reflecting her own wide, uncertain eyes. The room around her seemed to melt away, leaving her alone with the weight of Nikhil's proposal, the sheer enormity of his words echoing in the silence. Her past relationships flashed before her eyes, a parade of broken promises and unmet expectations. The ghosts of her insecurities, the deeply rooted fears she'd confessed to Nikhil in their virtual haven, rose up to meet her, whispering doubts and anxieties.

She had always been hesitant about commitment, a fear that stemmed not from a lack of desire, but from a deep-seated fear of heartbreak, a fear she'd meticulously crafted and carefully guarded through the years. Her virtual relationship with Nikhil had felt safe, a sanctuary from the complexities and potential pitfalls of a physical connection. But this…this was different. This was real, tangible, and terrifyingly significant.

She replayed the video, each word, each gesture, each heartfelt expression resonating with her on a deeper level. She had always admired Nikhil's sensitivity, his genuine empathy, his capacity for understanding, all those traits she had discovered and cherished through their digital interactions. Yet, despite all this, a shadow of doubt lingered, a lingering fear that the security of their virtual space might not translate to the unpredictable realities of a physical relationship.

She thought of their shared history, the countless hours spent creating a world together, a testament to their profound connection. She thought of the painstakingly crafted digital scavenger hunt, a symbol of his commitment, his dedication to their unique relationship. She thought of his gentle patience, his understanding, his unfailing support. She recalled his words about her strength, her resilience, her capacity for love; words that had affirmed her inherent worth in a way that no one ever had before.

But still, the hesitation persisted, a tremor of uncertainty that threatened to unravel the carefully built tapestry of her emotions. The fear of disappointment, the fear of repeating past mistakes, was a heavy cloak she couldn't quite shake off. It was a testament to the profound weight of her past experiences and the daunting prospect of embracing a future that felt both exhilarating and terrifyingly uncertain.

The silence in her room felt heavy, thick with unspoken anxieties and the weight of a life-altering decision. She was alone in her room, yet the space felt vast, echoing with the reverberations of Nikhil's proposal. The phone remained in her hand, the video frozen on his hopeful face, his earnest gaze questioning, waiting. The question hung in the air, unanswered, a cliffhanger of epic proportions, leaving the reader suspended between hope and apprehension, uncertain of the path that lay ahead for Charvi and Nikhil. The future of their digital love story hung precariously in the balance, a testament to the complexities of love, commitment, and the transition from the virtual to the real. The quiet anticipation was palpable, a tense silence broken only by the rhythm of Charvi's breath, as she grappled with the weight of his question, the weight of her own heart, and the uncertain future that lay before her. The simple question, "Will you marry me?", was transformed into a monumental decision, a crossroads that would determine the fate of their unique and extraordinary love story. The answer, however, remained elusive, shrouded in the quiet intensity of her contemplation, leaving the reader hanging on the edge of their seat, eager to witness the unfolding of this modern-day romance.

Charvis Decision 🖤

Her fingers traced the outline of the tiny, velvet box on her phone screen, the image of Nikhil's hopeful face frozen in time. The silence in her room was deafening, a stark contrast to the whirlwind of emotions raging within her. The weight of his proposal pressed down on her, a physical burden that made it hard to breathe. She replayed the video again, absorbing every nuance of his expression, every tremor in his voice. It wasn't just a proposal; it was a declaration of love, a testament to a connection that had blossomed in the unlikeliest of places – the digital world.

Tears welled in her eyes, not tears of sadness or fear, but tears of overwhelming emotion. A mixture of joy, apprehension, and a profound sense of gratitude washed over her. She had always been a cautious person, guarded by a wall of insecurities built over years of disappointing relationships. Each failed romance had chipped away at her faith in love, leaving her vulnerable and wary of commitment. Her virtual relationship with Nikhil had been a sanctuary, a safe space where she could be herself, free from the anxieties and judgments that had haunted her past.

But Nikhil had seen past her carefully constructed defenses. He had seen the real Charvi, the vulnerable, sometimes insecure woman hidden beneath the surface. He had accepted her flaws, celebrated her strengths, and loved her unconditionally, all within the confines of their digital world. And now, he was asking her to take a leap of faith, to step out of her comfort zone and embrace a future that was both exciting and terrifying.

She thought back to their first online encounter, a chance comment on a shared post that had sparked an unexpected connection. The initial hesitancy, the carefully worded messages, the gradual unveiling of their innermost selves – it all felt like a dream, a fantasy that was too beautiful to be real. Yet, here it was, tangible, undeniable, a testament to the power of connection in an increasingly digital world.

She remembered their virtual museum tours, their late-night chats that spilled over into the early hours of the morning, their shared laughter and tears, the silent understanding that existed between them, transcending the limitations of distance and technology. She recalled the intricate digital scavenger hunt he had painstakingly crafted, a symbol of his dedication, his unwavering commitment to their unique bond. It was a display of love and affection that surpassed any grand romantic gesture she had ever imagined.

And then there was the ring, simple and elegant, a perfect reflection of Nikhil's understated charm. It wasn't about the monetary value; it was about the symbolism, the representation of their extraordinary journey together. It was a tangible symbol of a love story that had unfolded not in the hustle and bustle of city life, but within the intimate sanctuary of their virtual world. A love story that had defied geographical boundaries, bridging continents and cultures with the simple power of human connection.

She considered the doubts, the fears that still lingered. The fear of failure, the fear of repeating past mistakes, the fear of jeopardizing something precious, something that felt too good to be true. These were valid fears, stemming from years of building walls to protect herself from heartbreak.

But Nikhil's love had chipped away at those walls, slowly,

patiently, gently revealing the woman she truly was, a woman capable of love, capable of commitment, capable of embracing the unknown.

She thought of the future, the uncertainties, the challenges that lay ahead. The transition from a virtual world to a physical reality would undoubtedly bring its own set of complexities and adjustments. But the thought of sharing her life with Nikhil, of experiencing the world with him by her side, filled her with a sense of exhilaration that overshadowed her fears. She imagined their future together, filled with adventures, shared laughter, mutual support, and an enduring love that transcended time and distance.

Her heart ached with a longing for him, a longing that transcended the digital divide. She yearned to feel his touch, to hear his voice in person, to share the mundane and extraordinary moments of life with him, not through a screen, but face-to-face.

A smile spread across her face, a smile that radiated warmth and happiness, a smile that reflected the love that bloomed within her heart. It was a smile that illuminated her room, banishing the shadows of doubt and insecurity that had once held her captive. The decision was made.

The fear was still there, a low hum beneath the surface, but it was now overshadowed by the immense joy and unwavering certainty in her heart.

She picked up her phone, her fingers trembling slightly as she typed a message. "Yes," she typed, the single word echoing the depth of her emotions. "Yes, a thousand times yes." She added a heart emoji, a simple symbol that encompassed the magnitude of her feelings.

She felt a sense of liberation, a release from the burden of her unspoken anxieties. She had made her decision, a decision that was both courageous and vulnerable, a decision that was an affirmation of her love for Nikhil, a declaration of her willingness to embrace a future that held both the promise of happiness and the possibility of heartache. But for now, all that mattered was the overwhelming joy, the exhilarating certainty of her heart, a heart that was overflowing with love.

She leaned back against her pillows, the weight of the decision lifted, replaced by a lightness that filled her with a sense of profound peace. She closed her eyes, picturing Nikhil's face, his eyes sparkling with happiness. She imagined holding his hand, walking side-by-side, sharing life's adventures, creating a future that was as unique and extraordinary as their love story. It was a future that began with a simple "yes," a yes that resonated with the depth of her heart, a yes that echoed through the digital divide, bridging the virtual and the real, connecting two souls bound by an extraordinary love. The journey ahead held both challenges and uncertainties, but she was ready to face them, hand-in-hand with Nikhil, her heart overflowing with love and hope. Their digital love story was about to transform into a tangible reality, a testament to the resilience of the human heart and the enduring power of love in all its forms. The future was uncertain, but one thing was clear: Charvi had chosen love, and in doing so, had chosen a future filled with untold possibilities.

First InPerson Meeting

The cafe buzzed with the low hum of conversation, the clinking of mugs, and the rhythmic whir of the espresso machine. Charvi sat nervously at a small table near the window, the late afternoon sun casting long shadows across the floor. She'd chosen this spot meticulously, a balance between being visible and having a degree of privacy. Her fingers fidgeted, twisting a stray strand of hair around her finger. She checked her phone for the tenth time in as many minutes, the screen illuminating her anxious face. She hadn't seen Nikhil's face except on her phone screen for the past year, a year filled with late-night conversations and shared dreams, a year that culminated in a proposal that still sent shivers down her spine.

The bell above the door chimed, announcing a new arrival, and her heart leaped into her throat. She looked up, her breath catching in her chest. There he was, Nikhil, stepping into the warm light of the cafe, even more handsome in person than in his countless video calls. He was just as she had imagined him, even more endearing. His smile, that infectious grin that had lit up her screen countless times, spread across his face as he spotted her. He looked even more stunning than in his photos, his eyes holding a depth that only a shared virtual year could create.

He approached the table, his gait a mixture of excitement and nervousness that mirrored her own. There was a brief moment of hesitation, a silent acknowledgment of the transition from virtual intimacy to the tangible reality of a face-to-face meeting. The air thrummed with unspoken anticipation, a mixture of joy and apprehension.

"Charvi," he said, his voice a soft melody that resonated deep within her. The sound of his voice, heard only through a speaker for so long, was now a physical sensation, a wave of warmth washing over her.

He pulled out the chair opposite her, his eyes never leaving hers. There was a palpable connection, an unspoken understanding that transcended the digital divide that had separated them for so long. He sat down, his presence filling the space between them, erasing the distance that had once seemed insurmountable.

"You look... even more beautiful than I imagined," he said, a blush rising on his cheeks. His words, simple yet profound, were a testament to the depth of their connection, a connection that had blossomed and flourished in the unlikeliest of circumstances.

Charvi blushed, her heart pounding in her chest. "You too," she managed to whisper, her voice barely audible above the cafe's gentle hum. She felt a wave of relief wash over her, the initial awkwardness dissolving as quickly as it had appeared. The nervousness she had felt earlier dissipated, replaced by a comfortable sense of familiarity. It was as though they had known each other for years, not just through pixels and screens, but through a shared journey of emotional discovery and intimate connection.

They ordered their coffees, their hands brushing accidentally as they reached for the menu. The brief touch sent a jolt of electricity through her, a tangible reminder of the physical connection that had been missing from their virtual relationship. They talked, effortlessly, easily, falling into a rhythm of conversation that felt both natural and intimate.

They spoke about their day, their work, their families, and their hopes and dreams. It wasn't a practiced conversation; it was a natural flow, a seamless blend of laughter, shared experiences, and unspoken understanding.

He spoke of his love for old films and classic literature, passions she had discovered through their countless virtual dates. She recounted her experiences volunteering at the local animal shelter, a detail he'd mentioned fondly during one of their late-night chats. The conversation was a testament to their shared interests and compatible personalities. They reminisced about their virtual museum tours, laughing at their inside jokes and shared memories from their virtual adventures. He described the painstaking effort that went into creating the digital scavenger hunt, revealing the thoughtful planning that went into every aspect of their virtual relationship. She confessed that his digital efforts had not only been romantic but had also been a catalyst for her courage to leave behind her protective shells of hesitancy and embrace the uncertainty of a real-life relationship.

As they sipped their coffees, they spoke of their hopes and fears regarding the transition from the digital to the physical world, acknowledging the challenges and adjustments that lay ahead. The prospect of navigating a long-distance relationship initially made them both nervous, but their shared conviction that their connection was strong enough to withstand any obstacles gave them both the strength to face the upcoming journeys together.

Charvi found herself captivated by his eyes, the warm brown depths that seemed to hold a universe of untold stories. He listened intently, his attention unwavering, making her feel seen, heard, and understood in a way she hadn't experienced in previous relationships. She spoke of her insecurities, her fears, the walls she had built around her heart, and he listened without judgment, offering words of encouragement and reassurance. His acceptance, his unconditional love, felt like a balm to her soul, a healing touch that eased the years of hurt and disappointment.

The hours slipped away, the cafe emptying around them, but their conversation flowed seamlessly, never faltering, never awkward. They spoke of their families, their aspirations, and their dreams for the future, their voices intertwining, creating a melody of shared hopes and aspirations. The initial nervousness had completely vanished, replaced by a comfortable intimacy that felt both natural and exhilarating.

As the sun began to set, casting a warm golden glow over the cafe, Nikhil reached across the table, his hand gently covering hers. The touch was soft, tender, sending a ripple of warmth through her veins. It was a gesture that transcended the simple act of physical contact; it was a symbol of their connection, their bond, a silent affirmation of their shared journey.

"I'm so glad I finally got to meet you," he said, his voice thick with emotion. His gaze held hers, and in that moment, she saw not just the man she had fallen in love with virtually but the man she was falling in love with in reality. The man she was destined to share her life with.

"Me too," she whispered, her voice choked with emotion. Tears welled in her eyes, tears of happiness, of relief, of overwhelming gratitude. Their first in-person meeting had exceeded all her expectations; it had been more beautiful, more real, more meaningful than she had ever dared to imagine.

They spent a few more moments in comfortable silence, their hands intertwined, the cafe's gentle hum providing a soothing backdrop to the silent understanding that passed between them. The transition from the virtual to the real world had been seamless, effortless, a testament to the strength of their connection. The digital bridge that had connected them for so long had been naturally replaced by the warm and comforting bridge of a real-life, passionate, loving relationship. The future held challenges, but as they walked out of the cafe, hand in hand, under the twilight sky, they both knew they were ready to face them together. The digital love story had blossomed into something tangible, something real, something extraordinary. Their journey together had only just begun.

Sweet Moments and Adventures 🖤🖤

Their first few months together were a whirlwind of laughter, shared secrets, and stolen kisses. It wasn't the grand, sweeping romance of novels; it was a quiet, blossoming love, unfolding organically and naturally. Their first official date wasn't in a fancy restaurant, but in a bustling park, sharing a picnic basket filled with their favorite foods, their conversation a lively mix of shared jokes and heartfelt confessions. The sun dappled through the leaves, casting dancing shadows on the checkered blanket they sat upon, a perfect backdrop to the growing affection between them. He told her stories of his childhood, his voice filled with a warmth that resonated deeply within her. She recounted her dreams, her hopes, her fears, feeling safe and understood in his presence, a feeling she hadn't experienced before. The simple act of sharing a meal, a laugh, a secret, felt profound, a testament to their burgeoning connection.

Their second date was at a classic movie theater, a place Nikhil had mentioned loving during one of their late-night virtual conversations. The old-fashioned charm of the place, the smell of popcorn, the shared anticipation of the film, created a sense of intimacy and connection. They held hands during the movie, their fingers intertwining, a silent acknowledgment of the physical connection that had been absent from their virtual relationship. The movie itself became secondary; it was the shared experience, the comfortable silence, the stolen glances, that truly mattered. Afterwards, they strolled along the quiet street, the night air filled with the sounds of crickets, the twinkling lights of the city casting a romantic glow on their faces. It was a simple date, yet it held a depth and significance that transcended the ordinary.

One Saturday, they went hiking through a nearby forest preserve, the sun warming their faces, the rustling leaves whispering secrets around them. The trail was challenging at times, forcing them to rely on each other for support, their hands brushing as they helped each other navigate the uneven path. The shared effort strengthened their bond, fostering a deeper connection. The beauty of the surrounding nature was a shared marvel, and they spent long moments in peaceful silence, simply appreciating the beauty of the forest and the comfortable companionship of each other. At one point, they stumbled upon a hidden waterfall, its cascading water creating a soothing melody. They paused, captivated by the beauty of nature, sharing a quiet moment of intimacy, their hands finding each other naturally. The shared

experience served to connect them further, as they expressed their feelings for each other, feelings so deep, so pure, so true.

Weekends were often spent exploring the city, discovering hidden cafes, exploring antique shops, and wandering through museums, places they'd discussed during their virtual dates. Each place held a new adventure, a new memory, a new story added to their evolving narrative. It was as though each location was a living testament to their growing bond. They explored hidden alleyways in the city, sharing spontaneous laughs and adventures, each exploration a unique treasure that served to add to their ever-growing collection of memories.

Evenings were often spent at each other's homes, curled

up on the couch, watching movies, or sharing stories, or simply enjoying each other's company. These moments felt safe, comfortable, intimate. These intimate moments, spent in the comforting warmth of their own homes, fostered a sense of belonging and security, of knowing that they could be truly themselves in each other's presence. The simple act of sharing a quiet evening, together, away from the outside world, helped establish a solid foundation of trust and companionship. The unspoken moments, the comfortable silences, were as powerful as their conversations.

They cooked together, their laughter filling the kitchen as they fumbled with recipes and spilled ingredients. The shared mess, the collaborative effort, became a source of joy and connection. They learned each other's culinary preferences, each shared meal a symbol of their growing bond. The meals they shared, often simple, home-cooked dishes, were an act of love and care, a symbol of their mutual respect for each other's feelings. The little imperfections only added to the charm.

One evening, while watching the sunset from Nikhil's balcony, he turned to her, his eyes sparkling with affection. He simply said, "I never thought I could find happiness like this, Charvi. Thank you." His words were heartfelt, genuine, and deeply touching. Her heart swelled with emotion, and tears welled up in her eyes. She had never imagined that a relationship that began virtually could lead to such a deep and profound love. It was then and there that she knew that she had indeed found her soulmate, a partner who cherished her for who she was, flaws and all.

Their relationship wasn't without its challenges. They had discussions, disagreements, moments of frustration. But even during these moments, their love and respect for each other shone through. They learned to communicate effectively, to navigate their differences with patience and understanding.

Their ability to resolve conflicts maturely and lovingly helped strengthen their bond further. The open and honest communication became a testament to their commitment and desire to build a lasting relationship.

The transition from a long-distance relationship to one where they saw each other regularly was a smooth one. Their connection was strong enough to withstand the challenges of physical proximity, the little annoyances, the everyday struggles of living together. They found joy in the small things – a shared cup of coffee in the morning, a spontaneous dance in the living room, a comforting hug after a long day.

Their relationship was full of warmth, acceptance and mutual respect.

They celebrated their first month anniversary with a candlelit dinner, a gesture that felt both simple and grand. They reminisced about their journey, from their first virtual encounter to their first in-person meeting, their laughter and tears intertwining as they relived the memories that had shaped their relationship. The meal was modest, but the love and celebration was immeasurable. The atmosphere was heartwarming, full of love, understanding and a promise for a beautiful future.

As the months passed, their love deepened, their bond strengthening with each shared experience, each quiet moment, each shared laughter. They created a world of their own, a sanctuary of love and understanding, amidst the chaos and uncertainties of life. Their relationship was a testament to the fact that even in the digital age, true love and connection could bloom, flourish and thrive. It was a story of two souls, connected by love, woven together by fate, and ready to face whatever the future held, together.

Their love story, born in the virtual world, had blossomed into something real, something tangible, something extraordinary – a love story for the ages.

Nikhils Surprise Visit

The afternoon sun cast long shadows across the manicured lawns of St. Mary's, dappling the ancient brick buildings in a warm, golden light. Charvi, engrossed in a particularly complex equation for her calculus assignment, barely registered the growing buzz around her. She was hunched over a weathered park bench beneath a sprawling oak tree, her brow furrowed in concentration, a half-eaten sandwich abandoned beside her notebook. The usual lunchtime chatter of students seemed muted, almost distant, a background hum to the mental gymnastics her brain was currently performing.

Suddenly, a shadow fell across her notes. She looked up, expecting to see a friend, perhaps offering a much-needed distraction. Instead, she found herself staring into Nikhil's eyes, his usual playful grin replaced with an expression of tender adoration. He stood there, a bouquet of sunflowers – her favorite – clutched in his hands, his eyes twinkling with mischief and affection. For a moment, time seemed to stop. The usual cacophony of the schoolyard faded, leaving only the sound of her own heart pounding against her ribs.

"Well, hello there, Professor," he said, his voice a low murmur that only she could hear, even amidst the surrounding hubbub. He presented her with the sunflowers, their bright faces mirroring the joy radiating from him.

Charvi's initial surprise morphed into a wide, disbelieving smile. A wave of warmth, a potent cocktail of astonishment, happiness, and sheer embarrassment washed over her. This was not how she expected to spend her lunch break. The calculus equation, previously her sole focus, vanished from her mind.

"Nikhil? What… what are you doing here?" she stammered, a blush creeping up her neck. He'd never visited her school before; their relationship, while deeply fulfilling, was carefully kept away from the prying eyes of her friends and classmates.

"I thought a little… surprise visit was in order," he replied, his voice a warm, comforting melody. He gently tucked a stray strand of hair behind her ear, a simple gesture that sent shivers down her spine. "I wanted to see where my brilliant girlfriend spends her days," he added, his eyes sparkling with affection.

Just then, her friends Priya and Maya emerged from behind a nearby bush, their faces a mixture of surprise and amusement. Priya, ever the drama queen, gasped theatrically. "Oh my god, Charvi! Is that… Nikhil?"

Maya, usually reserved, let out a delighted squeal. "He's even more handsome in person!"

The surprise was now a full-blown spectacle. Other students stopped to stare, their whispers creating a low murmur around the trio. Some giggled, others openly admired the charming Nikhil, while a few less-than-subtle glances toward Charvi were laced with a bit of envy.

Charvi felt her cheeks burn even brighter. She'd envisioned a quiet, intimate moment with Nikhil, perhaps a stolen kiss under the oak tree. This was… different. Much more public. And yet, despite the sudden spotlight, a wave of happiness washed over her, a feeling so profound it overshadowed any embarrassment. She loved that Nikhil was bold enough, loving enough to pull off this grand gesture.

Nikhil, unfazed by the growing audience, pulled out a small, neatly wrapped gift from his backpack. "This is for you," he said, handing it to her with a shy smile.

It was a small, leather-bound journal, its cover embossed with a delicate silver sunflower. Charvi's heart melted. This wasn't just a surprise visit; it was a thoughtfully planned, romantic gesture. This was him, showcasing his awareness of her interests and his understanding of the things that made her happy.

"It's beautiful," she breathed, opening the journal to reveal crisp, blank pages. "Thank you."

The rest of the lunch break was a blur of laughter, shared glances, and hushed conversations. Her friends peppered Nikhil with questions, their curiosity tempered with good- natured teasing. Nikhil handled it all with grace and humor, charming them with his easygoing nature and infectious smile. They were all caught up in the excitement of the moment, their initial shock giving way to delight and happy gossip.

As the bell rang, signaling the end of lunch, Nikhil took

her hand, his fingers interlacing with hers. The simple act felt immensely intimate, a silent promise amidst the school's boisterous energy.

"I'll see you later," he whispered, his breath ghosting across her cheek. The warmth of his touch lingered even after he released her hand.

The rest of the day passed in a happy daze. Charvi couldn't concentrate on her classes; her thoughts were constantly drifting back to Nikhil, to his surprise visit, his thoughtful gift, and the overwhelming joy his presence had brought her.

She relived the moment countless times, the laughter, the whispered conversations, the public display of affection. It was a memory she knew she would cherish forever.

Later that evening, they met at her favorite café. As they sipped on warm lattes, the conversation drifted naturally from the events of the day to their future plans, their hopes and dreams for their life together. The café, usually a place of quiet contemplation, felt infused with a vibrant energy, an electric current of love and anticipation. The casual setting didn't diminish the profound nature of their bond.

Nikhil confessed to a flutter of nerves before he'd shown up at her school. He'd envisioned a hundred different scenarios — her shock, her embarrassment, even her anger. He'd planned it all meticulously; his initial apprehension giving way to an almost reckless excitement to see her, to share that excitement with her, and to show his feelings for her in a tangible way.

He'd learned her class schedule through subtle inquiries, and spent the morning crafting the perfect surprise. He'd even discreetly gotten permission from the school principal, ensuring a smooth, if slightly unexpected, visit. His careful planning was a testament to the depth of his feelings, a careful orchestration of a romantic gesture that spoke volumes about his love for Charvi.

Charvi listened intently, her eyes mirroring the depth of her own love for him. His thoughtful planning, his meticulous attention to detail, his willingness to navigate potential embarrassment for the sake of showing her affection—it all spoke volumes of his devotion. His vulnerability, shared with such warmth and honesty, made him even more endearing. She felt a surge of love so profound, so overwhelming that tears welled up in her eyes.

They discussed the reactions of her friends, the amused glances of the other students, the sudden transformation of a regular lunchtime into a memory they would hold close to their hearts. They laughed about the unexpected nature of it all—the public display of affection, the shocked faces of her friends, the attention they'd received. It was an event that cemented their bond, their love story weaving itself into the fabric of their everyday lives.

That night, as they talked late into the night, nestled in the comfort of her own room, Charvi confessed that she'd initially been embarrassed by the public nature of the visit. Yet, despite her initial apprehension, the memory filled her with a profound sense of happiness. The thought of Nikhil, braving the schoolyard crowds to express his feelings so openly, filled her with warmth and a comforting sense of being cherished. His love wasn't shy; it was bold, brazen, and utterly irresistible. This wasn't just a surprise visit; it was a declaration of his love, loud and clear. And it had been perfect.

As days turned into weeks, the memory of Nikhil's surprise visit remained a cherished part of their story. It was a marker, a moment frozen in time, a testament to the unwavering bond they shared, a turning point in their evolving romance.

It was a story they would continue to share, an anecdote that brought smiles, laughter and a deeper appreciation for the unexpected ways love found its way into their lives. The sunflowers, long since wilted, were carefully pressed and kept in the front pages of her new leather-bound journal, a tangible reminder of the blossoming romance that had captured their hearts. The story of Nikhil's surprise visit was more than just a memory; it was a cornerstone of their love, a story that was just beginning to unfold.

Facing Parental Challenges 🖤🖤

The aroma of cardamom and cloves hung heavy in the air, a familiar comfort in Charvi's otherwise turbulent world. She sat perched on the edge of her bed, the worn leather of her new journal cool against her fingertips. The pressed sunflowers, a faded echo of Nikhil's grand gesture, lay nestled within its pages. The memory of that day, still vivid and vibrant, contrasted sharply with the heavy silence that had settled over her home since she'd told her parents about Nikhil.

Her parents, traditionally minded and deeply rooted in their cultural values, hadn't taken the news well. Their initial reaction had been a mixture of shock and disapproval, a storm of worried questions and disapproving glances that had left Charvi feeling both heartbroken and fiercely defensive. Their concerns, while rooted in a place of love and protectiveness, felt suffocating, a wall erected between her and the blossoming happiness she'd found with Nikhil.

Her mother, a woman of quiet strength and unwavering devotion to family tradition, had expressed concerns about Nikhil's background, his family's relatively modest means, and the perceived differences in their cultural upbringings. The subtle undertones of caste and class were hard to ignore, a painful reminder of societal pressures that Charvi had always tried to rise above.

Her father, a man of strong opinions and even stronger convictions, had voiced his anxieties about the timing. He felt their relationship was developing too quickly, too intensely, a whirlwind romance that threatened to derail Charvi's carefully planned future, a future meticulously mapped out by him with a specific trajectory in mind—a prestigious university, a stable career, and a suitable marriage within their community. He saw Nikhil as a distraction, a charming interlude that would ultimately lead to heartache.

The ensuing conversation had been a tumultuous blend of tears, raised voices, and firmly held beliefs. Charvi had defended Nikhil passionately, articulating the depth of her feelings, the unwavering commitment and mutual respect they shared. She'd tried to explain that their love transcended the superficial differences her parents fixated upon. She'd argued that Nikhil's kindness, intelligence, and ambition were far more significant than his socio-economic background.

But her words had fallen on deaf ears, her passion met with unyielding resistance. The chasm between her desires and her parents' expectations felt unbridgeable, a gulf of cultural differences and generational divides. The warmth and laughter of the café, the intimacy of their shared moments, seemed distant memories as she faced the cold reality of her parents' disapproval.

The following days had been filled with tense silences and strained interactions. Her mother had tried to subtly steer the conversation towards more "suitable" young men, suggesting potential suitors within their community—men who shared their cultural background, social standing, and family values. Her father, meanwhile, had increased his oversight of her studies, his anxieties manifesting as a stricter curfew and a greater emphasis on academic achievement. The atmosphere at home had transformed from one of loving support to one of watchful scrutiny, a constant reminder of the battle lines drawn.

Nikhil, understanding the sensitivity of the situation, had been supportive and patient, offering words of encouragement and reassurance. He hadn't pressured her to defy her parents, instead choosing to provide a quiet strength, a steady presence in the midst of her emotional turmoil. He'd visited her only once, a quiet evening spent on her porch, their conversation a low murmur amidst the rustling leaves of the ancient oak tree. They'd talked about their challenges, their hopes, and their dreams, clinging to the embers of their shared love amidst the storm raging within her family.

He suggested they write letters, a traditional way to maintain connection across distances, a form of communication that allowed them to express themselves without the immediate tension of face-to-face interaction. They'd exchanged heartfelt letters, written in the quiet hours of the night, pouring their hearts out onto paper, seeking comfort and understanding in the words they shared. His letters were filled with love, patience, and understanding. He reiterated his commitment to her, his resolve to navigate the challenges they faced together.

One evening, after a particularly tense dinner, Charvi

found herself staring out the window, the city lights blurring into a melancholic landscape. She thought about Nikhil's unwavering support, his understanding of her predicament, and his willingness to endure this period of uncertainty. His love wasn't a fleeting fancy; it was a deep commitment, a steadfast presence in the midst of the storm. It was a strength she needed to draw upon.

The next day, armed with a renewed sense of purpose, Charvi initiated a conversation with her parents. She didn't confront them; instead, she chose a path of calm explanation, a measured approach that aimed to bridge the gap between their differing perspectives. She acknowledged their concerns, validating their anxieties, but also highlighted the qualities that made Nikhil such a remarkable individual. She spoke not only of his character, but also his ambition, his plans for the future, and the love he shared for her.

She pointed out that love wasn't solely about matching cultural backgrounds or social standings; it was about mutual respect, shared values, and an unwavering commitment to build a life together. She explained that while she respected their traditions and beliefs, she couldn't sacrifice her own happiness to fulfill their expectations. She didn't demand their approval; she simply asked for their understanding. She shared her future aspirations, emphasizing that her academic goals would remain a priority, while making it clear that her happiness required acceptance of her relationship with Nikhil.

The conversation was long and emotionally charged, filled with moments of tense silence and tearful revelations. It was a painful process, a gradual unveiling of unspoken fears and carefully held beliefs. But slowly, subtly, a shift occurred.

Her mother, though still apprehensive, admitted to being impressed by Nikhil's resilience and determination. Her father, though maintaining a reserved demeanor, acknowledged Nikhil's genuine affection for Charvi and recognized the depth of their connection.

The breakthrough wasn't a complete acceptance; it was a gradual softening of their stance, a recognition that their daughter's happiness mattered. They agreed to meet Nikhil, a tentative first step towards building a bridge of understanding. It was a hard-won victory, but one that gave Charvi the courage to continue fighting for her love, for her future, and for the right to choose her own path. The battle wasn't over, but the first skirmish had been won, and the future, though still uncertain, held a glimmer of hope, a hint of the happiness that lay ahead. The sunflowers, a symbol of their blossoming romance, now held a different significance—a reminder of the resilience of their love, a promise of brighter days to come, a testament to the power of unwavering love in the face of parental challenges.

Navigating Family Conflicts 🖤

The meeting with Nikhil was set for a Sunday afternoon, a carefully chosen time to minimize disruption to their routines. Charvi spent the week meticulously preparing, trying to anticipate her parents' questions and rehearse answers that would assuage their concerns without compromising her own feelings. She cleaned her room obsessively, arranging her books and papers with a precision usually reserved for important exams. She even baked her mother's favorite cardamom-infused cookies, a small offering of peace, a gesture of goodwill.

Nikhil, ever the gentleman, arrived bearing a bouquet of lilies, their pristine white petals a stark contrast to the nervous energy buzzing within the small living room. Her father, sitting stiffly on the edge of the sofa, barely acknowledged his presence with a curt nod. Her mother, ever the observant one, studied him with a quiet intensity, her eyes scrutinizing his every move, his every word.

The initial awkwardness hung heavy in the air, the silence punctuated only by the ticking of the grandfather clock in the hallway. Charvi, acting as mediator, initiated the conversation, gently guiding the flow of dialogue, ensuring that everyone felt heard, respected, and understood. She spoke about Nikhil's passion for astronomy, his dedication to his studies, and his plans for the future – a future he now envisioned sharing with her.

Nikhil, in turn, spoke with a quiet confidence, acknowledging the cultural differences that existed but emphasizing the values they shared: hard work, honesty, and a deep-seated respect for family. He spoke of his admiration for Charvi's intelligence and strength, of his commitment to support her dreams, and of the unwavering love that bound them together. He didn't shy away from the challenges they faced, acknowledging the difficulties of navigating differing backgrounds, but expressed his willingness to bridge the gap, to learn, to adapt, and to grow together.

He brought along a portfolio showcasing his artwork – intricate astronomical charts rendered in vibrant watercolors. It was a testament to his talent, his passion, and his quiet ambition. His mother, a woman of refined tastes and a keen eye for art, found herself unexpectedly captivated by his skill. A slow, hesitant smile played on her lips as she examined his work, her initial reserve gradually melting away.

The conversation shifted from tense interrogation to a more relaxed exchange, a dialogue of mutual respect and understanding. Her father, though still reserved, participated more actively, asking questions about Nikhil's family, his aspirations, and his vision for the future. He asked about Nikhil's parents, their professions, and their views on their son's relationship with Charvi. Nikhil answered with honesty and transparency, detailing his family's history, their values, and their unwavering support for his relationship with Charvi.

Nikhil's respectful demeanor, his quiet confidence, and his thoughtful responses gradually eased the tension in the room. He spoke about his own family's values, emphasizing the importance of hard work, integrity, and mutual respect – values that surprisingly resonated with Charvi's parents' own. He spoke of his dreams, not just of personal success, but also of building a family life grounded in love and mutual support. He spoke of his respect for Charvi's heritage and his willingness to learn about and appreciate her culture.

He didn't attempt to downplay the differences between their backgrounds; rather, he presented them as opportunities for growth, for learning, for expanding their horizons. He articulated his commitment to building bridges, to understanding and appreciating both of their cultural heritage. He emphasized that love transcended superficial differences, that their bond was rooted in shared values, mutual respect, and an unwavering commitment to each other.

The afternoon flowed by more smoothly than Charvi had dared to hope. The initial apprehension slowly gave way to a sense of cautious optimism. By the end of the meeting, a tangible shift had occurred. While complete acceptance wasn't immediate, a palpable sense of understanding replaced the earlier animosity. There was a grudging respect for Nikhil, a recognition of his character and his commitment to Charvi.

Her mother, ever the pragmatic one, began discussing practical matters, inquiring about Nikhil's plans for the future, his career aspirations, and his approach to life. This transition from questioning to planning was a significant step forward. Her father, though still holding back somewhat, offered a nod of approval, a tacit acceptance that was more meaningful than any explicit declaration.

The meeting concluded with a tentative agreement – a plan for a family dinner in the coming weeks, an opportunity to further build bridges and cultivate deeper connections. It was a small step, but a significant one, a testament to the power of communication, understanding, and a shared commitment to overcoming obstacles. As Nikhil stood to leave, he exchanged a warm, reassuring smile with Charvi, a silent acknowledgment of their victory, a shared understanding of the journey ahead.

The following days were filled with a more relaxed atmosphere at home. The strained silences were replaced by more natural conversations, the watchful scrutiny replaced by a gentler curiosity. Charvi found herself sharing more freely with her parents, discussing her day, her classes, her future aspirations, and, of course, Nikhil. Her mother began offering subtle gestures of support, offering words of encouragement, and even helping Charvi prepare for upcoming exams.

Her father, though still maintaining a certain level of

reservedness, made an effort to engage with Nikhil directly, sending messages and offering subtle indications of acceptance. He started asking Nikhil about his work, and even offered some advice about navigating the challenges of his field of study. This newfound engagement felt like a monumental shift from his previous antagonism. The shift in their relationships was subtle, a slow but significant change that marked a turning point in the family dynamic.

One evening, while helping Charvi with her studies, her father even shared a story from his younger days, a glimpse into his past that allowed Charvi to understand him better, to see him not just as the stern authority figure, but also as a man with his own dreams, struggles, and vulnerabilities. The shared laughter that evening, a rare and precious commodity, felt like a victory, a celebration of the delicate progress they had made.

The road ahead wasn't without its bumps and obstacles. Cultural differences still existed, and the challenges of blending two distinct worlds into one remained. But the atmosphere of suspicion and disapproval had been replaced by a hesitant acceptance, a cautious optimism that paved the way for a more harmonious future. The sunflowers, their petals now slightly drooping but still holding onto their vibrant color, were a potent symbol of their enduring love, a reminder of the resilience of their commitment, and a testament to the power of understanding and perseverance in the face of conflict. Their blossoming romance was not just about two people falling in love, but also about two families, two worlds, slowly learning to understand and accept each other. The future, though still uncertain, held a new promise—a promise of shared joy, family acceptance, and a love story strengthened by the trials it had overcome.

Compromise and Understanding ♥♥

The tentative agreement reached at the initial meeting proved to be a crucial stepping stone. The planned family dinner, initially a source of anxiety for Charvi, became a surprisingly positive experience. Nikhil, armed with a thoughtful gift – a beautifully bound collection of Indian folk tales – and a sincere desire to connect, charmed Charvi's extended family. He listened attentively to stories of their heritage, asking insightful questions and demonstrating a genuine interest in their traditions. He even attempted, with admirable enthusiasm, a few phrases in Hindi, earning a warm chuckle from Charvi's grandmother, a woman known for her discerning eye and even more discerning standards.

The dinner wasn't without its moments of quiet tension. Certain cultural nuances, unspoken expectations, and subtle differences in communication style created occasional silences and slightly awkward exchanges. However, Nikhil's willingness to learn, his evident respect for their traditions, and his genuine affection for Charvi gradually chipped away at the initial resistance. He engaged in lively conversations about everything from astrophysics (a subject that fascinated Charvi's uncle, a retired physics professor) to the merits of different spice blends (a topic that captivated her aunt, a renowned home cook). He even managed to hold his own in a spirited debate on the relative merits of Bollywood versus Hollywood films with Charvi's cousin, a self-proclaimed film critic.

The evening ended with a sense of shared laughter and a surprising warmth. Charvi's father, who had remained somewhat reserved throughout the evening, surprised everyone by offering a toast to the couple, a brief but heartfelt acknowledgement of their burgeoning relationship. His words, though few, carried a weight of acceptance that resonated deeply with Charvi. The subtle shift in his demeanor, the softening of his gaze, was a testament to Nikhil's efforts and the unwavering strength of Charvi's love.

Following the dinner, the relationship between Nikhil and Charvi's family continued to evolve. Nikhil took the initiative to learn more about their cultural traditions,

attending local festivals and events, immersing himself in the vibrant tapestry of their heritage. He enthusiastically participated in Holi celebrations, his face smeared with vibrant colors, a stark contrast to his usually reserved demeanor. He even tried his hand at making traditional Indian sweets with Charvi's mother, enduring a slightly chaotic but ultimately enjoyable culinary adventure. These shared experiences, seemingly small and insignificant in isolation, cumulatively strengthened the bonds between Nikhil and Charvi's family, fostering a deeper sense of understanding and mutual respect.

Charvi, in turn, found herself becoming more open and communicative with Nikhil about her family's expectations and anxieties. She shared stories of her childhood, her aspirations, and her deepest fears, allowing Nikhil to understand the complexities of her background and the emotional weight she carried. They talked openly about their differences, their challenges, and their dreams for the future, creating a safe space for honest and vulnerable conversations. They learned to navigate their distinct cultural backgrounds, appreciating their unique perspectives while embracing their shared values.

One Saturday afternoon, while strolling through a bustling farmers market, Nikhil surprised Charvi with a small gift – a hand-painted terracotta pot adorned with intricate floral designs. It was a simple gesture, yet it spoke volumes about his growing understanding of her heritage. The pot, a symbol of their shared journey, became a cherished keepsake, a reminder of their blossoming relationship and the bridges they were building together.

Their relationship wasn't without its struggles. Occasional misunderstandings arose, rooted in their differing cultural backgrounds and communication styles. There were times when patience wore thin, when frustrations boiled over, and when the weight of expectations threatened to overwhelm them. But through it all, they held onto their commitment, their unwavering love serving as an anchor in the storm.

They learned to compromise, to find common ground, to adapt to each other's needs. They developed a unique vocabulary of gestures, expressions, and inside jokes, a private language that transcended the barriers of language and culture. They discovered a shared love for old movies, spending countless evenings curled up on the couch, watching classic films and discussing their favorite scenes, their laughter echoing through the quiet rooms of Charvi's home.

One evening, while discussing their future plans, Charvi opened up to Nikhil about her apprehension about leaving for college in a different city. She expressed her fears of being far from her family, and Nikhil, with a gentle touch and a warm embrace, reassured her, promising to make frequent visits and to always be there for her, no matter the distance. His words, coupled with his steadfast support, eased her anxiety, strengthening the foundation of their relationship.

Their bond grew stronger with each shared experience, each overcome challenge, each act of kindness and understanding.

They were not merely lovers; they were partners, co-navigators on a shared journey of self-discovery and mutual growth. Their love story wasn't a fairy tale, but a testament to the enduring power of human connection, the strength of compromise, and the resilience of a love built on mutual respect and understanding. They were creating a life together, a tapestry woven with threads of their unique heritage and their shared dreams, a life that would be both distinctly theirs and deeply connected to the families and cultures that shaped them.

The sunflowers, once a symbol of their budding romance, now stood tall and proud, their vibrant yellow petals a testament to their enduring love, their resilience in the face of adversity, and their unwavering commitment to each other. The journey wasn't over, but they were walking hand in hand, their steps synchronized, their hearts beating as one. The future, once a daunting landscape filled with uncertainty, now appeared as a boundless horizon, filled with the promise of shared joy, mutual support, and a love story stronger and more meaningful than either had ever imagined. The compromise and understanding they had cultivated were not just about bridging cultural divides; they were about building a foundation for a lifelong partnership, a testament to the power of love's ability to overcome obstacles and blossom into something truly extraordinary.

Building Bridges with Family 🖤🖤

The following weeks were a delicate dance of cautious optimism and persistent effort. Nikhil understood that winning over Charvi's parents wouldn't happen overnight. It required patience, understanding, and a willingness to embrace their world, not just expect them to embrace his. He started small. He learned to make chai exactly to her mother's exacting specifications, a feat that earned him a surprisingly warm smile and a whispered compliment about his "remarkable dedication." He helped her father with his meticulous gardening, their shared silence punctuated only by the gentle rustle of leaves and the chirping of birds. These seemingly insignificant acts, performed with genuine sincerity, were subtly altering the dynamics within the family.

One evening, Charvi's mother invited him to join them for

a family game night. It was a surprisingly boisterous affair, filled with the competitive spirit and playful banter that characterized their close-knit family. Nikhil, initially hesitant, found himself swept up in the joyful chaos. He laughed along with their jokes, even managing to win a particularly fierce game of carrom, earning him another round of surprised, and ultimately approving, glances. It was during this seemingly inconsequential game night that a genuine connection began to blossom. He wasn't just Charvi's boyfriend; he was becoming a part of their family, however tentatively.

The next significant step involved a family trip to Charvi's ancestral village. It was a deeply significant event for Charvi and her family, a pilgrimage to their roots, a celebration of their heritage. Nikhil, despite his initial apprehension about navigating an unfamiliar cultural landscape, approached the trip with open arms and an eagerness to learn. He listened intently to the elders' stories, absorbing the history and traditions passed down through generations. He participated wholeheartedly in the village festivities, engaging in the traditional dances and rituals with an infectious enthusiasm. He even attempted to prepare a local delicacy, albeit with slightly disastrous results, which brought peals of laughter from the entire family. His clumsy attempts, his willingness to participate and learn, spoke volumes about his commitment to Charvi and her family.

His efforts weren't always met with immediate acceptance. There were still moments of hesitation, subtle reservations, and the occasional pointed question from Charvi's father, who remained a bastion of careful observation. But the resistance was softening, becoming less a wall and more of a slightly ajar door. He noticed that her father's critical gaze was slowly becoming less critical, replaced by a quieter scrutiny, a careful assessment of his character. He saw it in the subtle ways her father would offer him a cup of tea, in the brief, almost imperceptible nods of approval during conversations. These were small victories, but significant nonetheless.

Charvi played an integral role in this reconciliation process. She acted as a bridge, translating unspoken sentiments, explaining cultural nuances, and fostering understanding between Nikhil and her family. She patiently addressed their concerns, acknowledging their reservations, and highlighting Nikhil's genuine efforts to connect with them. She often shared anecdotes from their time together, showcasing his kindness, his humor, and his genuine affection for her. She deftly navigated the complexities of their differing perspectives, ensuring that neither side felt misunderstood or marginalized.

One afternoon, Charvi's grandmother, a woman known for her wisdom and unwavering standards, took Nikhil aside for a private conversation. Initially, he was nervous, anticipating a stern lecture or a critical assessment. Instead, she shared stories of her own youth, of her own love story, of the challenges and compromises she and her husband faced as they built their life together. She spoke of the importance of understanding, of respecting cultural differences, and of the enduring power of love to overcome even the most formidable obstacles. It was a deeply personal conversation, a testament to her acceptance, a quiet blessing on their burgeoning relationship.

The turning point came during a family Diwali celebration. The festival, typically associated with vibrant colors, dazzling lights, and joyous festivities, was initially tinged with a sense of apprehension for Nikhil. However, he surprised everyone with his thoughtful contribution – a meticulously crafted rangoli design at the entrance of the house, a beautiful and intricate work of art depicting the intertwined roots of two different cultures. It was a powerful visual metaphor for the bridge he was building between their two worlds. The look on her father's face as he gazed at the rangoli, a quiet mixture of pride and acceptance, spoke volumes.

That night, as the family gathered around the bonfire, sharing stories and laughter, Charvi's father approached Nikhil, his demeanor relaxed and his eyes holding a newfound warmth. He extended his hand, a gesture of acceptance that went far beyond words. He spoke about his initial reservations, his concerns about the future, but acknowledged Nikhil's unwavering commitment and genuine efforts to bridge the cultural gap. He spoke of the importance of respecting tradition, but also of embracing the evolving nature of relationships and family. His words, heartfelt and sincere, were a testament to the slow, gradual, but ultimately successful effort to build a bridge of understanding.

The journey wasn't without its further bumps. There were still occasional misunderstandings, moments of friction, and the lingering shadow of cultural differences. But the foundation had been laid, the bridge had been built. The relationship between Nikhil and Charvi's family continued to evolve, strengthened by shared experiences, mutual respect, and a growing sense of belonging. Nikhil became an integral part of their lives, a welcomed addition to their family circle. He wasn't just Charvi's boyfriend; he was their son, their friend, a part of their extended family, a testament to the power of love, understanding, and the unwavering commitment to build bridges, not walls. The sunflowers, once a symbol of their budding romance, now bloomed brightly amidst a landscape of shared happiness, reflecting the resilience of their love and the strength of the family bonds they had painstakingly forged. The future stretched before them, a shared journey filled with promise, laughter, and the comforting warmth of family.

Strengthening Their Bond 🖤🖤

The quiet hum of the city faded as Nikhil and Charvi retreated to their sanctuary – a small, sun-drenched apartment overlooking a bustling marketplace. It was their haven, a space where the pressures of family expectations and cultural differences momentarily dissolved, replaced by the simple comfort of each other's presence. Here, amidst the gentle aroma of brewing coffee and the soft melodies drifting from Charvi's old record player, they carved out moments of intimacy and connection. It wasn't always easy; the lingering anxieties about her family's acceptance still cast a long shadow, even in their private moments.

One evening, while curled up on the worn sofa, Nikhil noticed a flicker of sadness in Charvi's eyes. He gently reached for her hand, his touch sending a ripple of warmth through her. "What's wrong, my love?" he asked softly, his voice laced with concern.

Charvi sighed, her gaze drifting towards the window. "It's just… sometimes I feel like I'm walking a tightrope," she confessed, her voice barely a whisper. "Trying to balance my family's expectations with my own desires, my own dreams. And I worry that I'm not doing a good enough job."

Nikhil pulled her closer, his embrace offering solace and understanding. "You're doing amazing, Charvi," he reassured her, his voice firm but gentle. "You're navigating a complex situation with grace and strength. Don't forget that."

He understood her anxieties. He had witnessed firsthand the subtle pressures she faced, the delicate balancing act she performed daily. He knew that her desire to bridge the gap between her family and him came at a cost, a constant negotiation between her loyalty and her love. He wanted to alleviate her burden, to share the weight she carried.

"We'll face it together," he promised, his gaze locking with hers. "We'll find a way to make them understand, to show them that our love isn't just a fleeting phase, but something real, something strong, something worth fighting for."

Their conversations weren't always filled with grand pronouncements or sweeping gestures of romance. Instead, their bond deepened through small, intimate moments – shared laughter over silly movies, quiet evenings spent reading side-by-side, heart-to-heart talks whispered under the blanket of the night sky. They learned to communicate not just through words, but through gestures, through shared glances, through the silent understanding that blossomed between them. They celebrated their differences, finding joy in their contrasting personalities and perspectives. He learned to appreciate her traditional values, while she embraced his modern outlook. They discovered that their contrasting backgrounds weren't obstacles, but rather enriching aspects of their relationship, a vibrant tapestry woven from different threads.

One weekend, they decided to embark on a spontaneous adventure, escaping the city's clamor for the tranquility of a nearby hill station. The crisp mountain air, the breathtaking vistas, and the quiet solitude provided the perfect backdrop for introspection and reconnection. They hiked through lush forests, their conversations flowing effortlessly, their laughter echoing through the trees. They shared their fears, their dreams, their hopes for the future. They rediscovered the joy of simply being together, away from the complexities of their lives, letting their love be the guiding star.

The trip wasn't just a romantic getaway; it was a testament to their resilience, their ability to face challenges head-on, and their unwavering commitment to their relationship. It reaffirmed their shared vision, their understanding of their shared path. The conversations they had amidst the beauty of the hills solidified their commitment to each other, reinforcing their understanding and strengthening their bond. It was a reminder that their love was strong enough to withstand the storms that life threw their way.

Back in the city, they continued to navigate the complexities of their lives, learning to appreciate the quiet moments, the simple gestures, the profound impact of unspoken words.

They discovered that true strength lay not in avoiding conflict, but in their ability to resolve it, to understand each other's perspectives, and to compromise without compromising their individual identities. Arguments arose, naturally, but they learned to communicate effectively, to address their concerns respectfully, and to find solutions that honored both their needs.

Nikhil learned to express his emotions more openly, acknowledging his vulnerabilities without fear. Charvi, in turn, embraced her independence, asserting her opinions without hesitation. Their relationship evolved into a harmonious dance of mutual respect, understanding, and unwavering support. They were two distinct individuals, each with their own dreams, their own passions, yet they were inextricably intertwined, their lives interwoven in a beautiful tapestry of love and shared experiences.

One evening, as they were sharing a quiet dinner, Charvi confessed her anxieties about an upcoming family gathering. "My uncle is notoriously difficult," she sighed, her voice laced with apprehension. "He's known for his sharp wit and his even sharper tongue."

Nikhil smiled reassuringly, his hand gently covering hers. "We'll face it together," he repeated, his voice firm and steady. "We've overcome bigger obstacles, haven't we?"

He had a plan. He had spent weeks studying her family's cultural nuances, learning about their traditions and values. He wanted to show them, not just tell them, that he was committed to being a part of their world. He wanted to be more than just Charvi's boyfriend; he wanted to earn their respect, their trust, their acceptance.

The following weeks were filled with preparations. Nikhil immersed himself in the details of the upcoming family event, learning about the intricate rituals, the traditional dishes, and the expected customs. He even sought guidance from Charvi's relatives, asking insightful questions and demonstrating his sincere interest in their traditions. He was meticulous in his preparations, determined to demonstrate his sincerity and respect. His efforts were not just about winning over her family; they were about demonstrating the depth of his love for Charvi and his commitment to their future.

He spent hours researching and practicing a traditional dance, a dance that represented the heart of her culture. He knew it wouldn't be perfect, but his effort would convey his respect. He spent additional hours learning to prepare a particular dish that was a family favorite, a dish that required patience and precision. He practiced until his hands were sore, until his movements were almost fluid, his intent clearly defined. He was proving to them, to Charvi, to himself, that he was invested in their life, in their culture, in their future.

When the day of the family gathering finally arrived, Nikhil wasn't just another guest; he was a participant, a welcomed addition. His thoughtful gifts, his genuine interest in the conversations, his graceful participation in the traditional dance, all spoke volumes about his dedication. His willingness to embrace her culture, his genuine effort to learn and understand, his obvious love and respect for her family, slowly chipped away at the resistance that had once been there.

He didn't just bridge the cultural gap; he built a bridge of love, understanding, and mutual respect. The sunflower seeds that once symbolized their burgeoning romance had blossomed into a vibrant field, a testament to the strength of their bond, a symbol of their triumphant journey. Their future, once clouded by uncertainty, now shone bright with the promise of a life shared, a family united, and a love that had conquered all obstacles. Their story, still unfolding, was a testament to the enduring power of love, understanding, and unwavering commitment.

Supporting Each Others Dreams 🖤

The aroma of freshly brewed chai filled their small apartment, a comforting counterpoint to the anxieties swirling in Charvi's mind. She was staring at her laptop screen, a half-finished design sketch mocking her from the glowing pixels. Her dream of opening her own sustainable fashion label felt further away than ever, the weight of her family's expectations pressing down on her like a physical burden. The pressure to secure a stable, "respectable" job in a traditional field was a constant undercurrent in her life, a subtle but persistent dissonance against the melody of her own aspirations.

Nikhil, sensing her distress, gently placed a steaming mug in her hands. He didn't need words; their silent communication had evolved into a language all its own. He knew the sleepless nights, the self-doubt, the agonizing internal debate between duty and desire. He had seen the spark of frustration dim in her eyes more than once.

"It's not working," she murmured, her voice barely audible above the gentle hum of the city outside. "The designs...they just don't feel right. I feel like I'm forcing it, trying to fit into a mold that isn't mine."

Nikhil leaned against the countertop, his gaze unwavering. "Tell me about it," he urged gently. "What's not working?

What's missing?"

He didn't offer solutions; he offered a safe space, a listening ear, a shoulder to lean on. He knew the best way to help wasn't to impose his perspective, but to understand hers, to validate her feelings, to help her find her own way through the maze of doubt and uncertainty. He listened as she poured out her frustrations, her anxieties, her fears of failure, her fear of disappointing her family. He listened without judgment, without interruption, his presence a comforting anchor in her storm.

As she spoke, he noticed a pattern emerging—a disconnect between her design concepts and her true inspiration. Her designs, while technically proficient, lacked the vibrant energy, the unique soul that he knew resonated within her.

Her family's expectations, he realized, were inadvertently stifling her creative spirit, forcing her to compromise her vision for something perceived as more "practical."

"Maybe," Nikhil began cautiously, choosing his words carefully, "maybe you're trying too hard to please everyone else. Maybe you need to reconnect with what truly inspires you. What makes your heart sing?"

Charvi was silent for a moment, her gaze fixed on the swirling steam rising from her chai. Then, a faint smile touched her lips. "You're right," she admitted softly. "I've been so focused on what others expect, I've forgotten what I actually want. I need to go back to the basics, to the things that originally sparked my passion."

That night, they embarked on a creative journey together. They flipped through vintage magazines, exploring textile patterns and color palettes. They visited local markets, immersing themselves in the vibrant textures and colors of traditional fabrics. They talked, they brainstormed, they laughed, they rediscovered the joy of collaborative creation. Nikhil, despite his lack of design background, became her invaluable sounding board, offering thoughtful suggestions, challenging her assumptions, and helping her refine her vision.

His support wasn't just emotional; it was practical too. He helped her research sustainable materials, connect with ethical suppliers, and navigate the complexities of setting up a small business. He managed the financial aspects, meticulously tracking expenses and income, ensuring her vision wouldn't crumble under the weight of administrative burdens. He understood that supporting her dream meant supporting her in every aspect, not just emotionally but practically.

Meanwhile, Nikhil's own dreams were also unfolding. He was determined to pursue his passion for environmental advocacy. He had been volunteering with local environmental groups for months, but now, he envisioned something bigger, a more substantial contribution. He planned to start an online platform dedicated to educating and engaging young people on climate change and sustainable living. This was a daunting task, but Charvi was his unwavering champion.

She spent countless hours helping him refine his website design, creating engaging content, and connecting him with potential partners and collaborators. She became his social media manager, strategist, and most importantly, his cheerleader. She understood the importance of his work, recognizing it not just as his personal passion but as a crucial endeavor for their future. She saw the dedication in his eyes, the fire in his heart, and her love amplified his determination.

Their evenings were filled with the clatter of keyboards, the murmurs of brainstorming sessions, and the shared exhilaration of progress. They celebrated each milestone, each small victory, with heartfelt hugs and shared dreams for the future. They learned that supporting each other's dreams wasn't just about individual success, it was about building a shared future, a future where their individual passions intersected, complemented, and strengthened their bond.

Their apartment, once just a haven from the outside world, transformed into a vibrant hub of creativity and collaboration. Sketches, fabric swatches, and program code littered their table, testament to their shared aspirations.

They navigated the inevitable challenges – technical glitches, creative blocks, and moments of self-doubt – together, their combined strength and unwavering support proving to be their most valuable assets. The quiet hum of their shared efforts became the soundtrack of their love story, a symphony of mutual respect and unwavering commitment.

One evening, after a particularly grueling workday, Nikhil collapsed onto the sofa, exhaustion etched on his face. "I'm not sure I can do this," he confessed, his voice laced with frustration. "The website is taking longer than expected, and the funding is still uncertain. I'm starting to doubt myself."

Charvi, ever perceptive, immediately sensed his discouragement. She sat beside him, her hand gently caressing his arm. "You're doing amazing, Nikhil," she reassured him, her voice soft but firm. "Don't let the challenges overshadow your progress. Remember why you started this, remember the impact you want to make. You're making a difference, even if you don't see it yet."

She reminded him of all the small victories they had already achieved, the positive feedback they had received, the growing community of supporters. She helped him refocus, reminding him of the purpose behind his work, the positive change he aspired to create. She didn't offer empty platitudes; she offered genuine encouragement, grounded in the reality of their shared journey.

Their support extended beyond the realm of personal

pursuits. They faced the inevitable challenges of balancing their personal lives with their ambitious goals. There were days of late nights, missed movie dates, and the occasional exhaustion-fueled argument. But through it all, their commitment to each other remained unshaken. They learned to communicate their needs, to prioritize their time effectively, and to make conscious choices that honored both their individual aspirations and their shared relationship.

Their mutual support wasn't a passive act; it was an active, ongoing process. They were each other's anchors, their safe harbors, their cheerleaders, and their partners in crime. Their journey was far from over, their dreams still unfolding, but the strength of their bond, forged in shared struggles and celebrated victories, promised a future bright with possibilities. Their story was a testament to the power of mutual support, a resounding affirmation that love and ambition could indeed coexist, flourishing in the fertile ground of shared dreams and unwavering commitment.

Facing External Pressures 💕

The next Friday evening found them at a bustling rooftop bar, a gathering of friends celebrating Priya's promotion. Priya, a whirlwind of energy and ambition, had always been Charvi's closest confidante, yet lately, their conversations had taken a subtly different tone. Priya, secure in her corporate career, often voiced her concerns about Charvi's and Nikhil's unconventional paths. "Are you sure about this, Charvi?" she'd ask, her tone laced with a mixture of concern and skepticism. "It's all very…romantic, but what if it doesn't work out? You're risking so much."

Tonight, amidst the clinking glasses and lively chatter, Priya's anxieties bubbled to the surface again. "You know, sometimes I wonder if you're both being a little naive," Priya said, her voice lowered to be heard only by Charvi.

"A sustainable fashion label and an environmental advocacy platform? It's all so… idealistic. The real world isn't so kind to dreamers."

Charvi felt a familiar pang of self-doubt. Priya's words weren't malicious, but they struck a chord, echoing the unspoken concerns she sometimes harbored herself. Nikhil, sensing her shift in mood, subtly squeezed her hand under the table. He knew the subtle pressures Charvi faced from her own family, and now, this added layer of external validation was proving challenging.

"It's not about being naive, Priya," Nikhil interjected, his voice calm and measured. "It's about pursuing what we're passionate about. It's about creating something meaningful, something that aligns with our values. We're not ignoring the challenges; we're facing them head-on, together."

The conversation shifted, the initial tension dissipating under Nikhil's assuredness. He skillfully steered the topic towards Priya's own accomplishments, celebrating her success while subtly highlighting the different paths to fulfillment. He acknowledged the risks they were taking but emphasized the potential rewards, not just financial, but personal and societal. He painted a picture of a future where their dreams intertwined, creating a ripple effect of positive change.

Later, as they walked home, hand in hand, Charvi confessed her lingering anxieties. "Priya's right, you know," she admitted, her voice soft. "It's terrifying. What if we fail? What if this doesn't work?"

Nikhil stopped walking, pulling her close. "Failing doesn't mean we've wasted our time," he said, looking into her eyes. "It means we tried, we learned, and we grew. And we'll do it together. That's what matters." He kissed her forehead, his touch conveying a sense of unwavering support that calmed her immediate fears.

The following weeks brought their own set of external pressures. Charvi's parents, initially supportive of her entrepreneurial spirit, began expressing increasing concern as deadlines loomed and financial projections remained uncertain. Their subtle disapproval—packaged in concerned phone calls and well-meaning but pointed questions— created a simmering tension beneath the surface of their family gatherings.

Nikhil, too, faced hurdles. Securing funding for his environmental platform proved more challenging than anticipated, and the constant rejection emails chipped away at his confidence. He found himself spending long hours alone, wrestling with doubts and anxieties, the weight of his aspirations pressing heavily on his shoulders.

One particularly draining evening, after a string of disappointing grant applications, Nikhil retreated to their small apartment, his usual optimism replaced by a palpable sense of defeat. Charvi, sensing his despair, found him hunched over his laptop, the glow of the screen illuminating the lines of exhaustion etched on his face.

"Tell me what's wrong," she urged, sitting beside him.

He poured out his frustration, his voice cracking with emotion. The pressure of his ambition, the constant rejection, and the fear of letting her down had overwhelmed him.

Charvi listened patiently, offering not empty reassurances, but empathetic understanding. She reminded him of his progress, his dedication, the positive impact he was already making, however small. She reaffirmed her faith in him and his vision.

Their response to these external pressures was not to retreat, but to confront them together. They sought guidance from mentors and advisors, learning to navigate the complexities of business and funding. They strengthened their communication, their shared vulnerabilities forging a deeper bond. They redefined their boundaries, learning to prioritize their well-being amidst the demands of their ambitions.

They also learned to seek support beyond each other. They joined local entrepreneurs' groups, connecting with others navigating similar challenges, finding comfort and encouragement in shared experiences. They attended workshops on stress management and work-life balance, strengthening their coping mechanisms and strategies for managing their workload. They learned that their success wasn't solely dependent on their individual efforts but on building a supportive network around them.

The pressures remained, but their response evolved. Instead of feeling defeated, they learned to view challenges as opportunities for growth, for refinement, for strengthening their bond. Their relationship, once a sanctuary from the outside world, became a source of strength, resilience, and unwavering support. They learned to redefine success not just in terms of financial achievements or professional milestones, but in terms of the journey, the growth, and the enduring strength of their shared commitment. The external pressures, once a threat to their dreams, became the crucible that forged an even stronger bond between them, solidifying their shared future and their unwavering love for one another. They learned that sometimes, the greatest victories aren't won in isolation, but in shared struggle, mutual support, and an unwavering belief in each other's potential. And that, perhaps, was the most valuable lesson of all.

Planning the
Wedding 💕

The initial euphoria of their engagement slowly gave way to the whirlwind of wedding planning. It started with a shared Pinterest board, overflowing with images of rustic chic venues, cascading floral arrangements, and dreamy, ethereal gowns. The board, initially a source of amusement and playful debate, quickly morphed into a visual representation of the immense task ahead. Choosing a date felt monumental, a decision weighing heavily on the calendar, mindful of family availability and the peak season for wedding venues. Securing a venue, a charming vineyard nestled in rolling hills an hour outside the city, felt like winning a lottery – a testament to their meticulous planning and a dash of luck.

The next few weeks blurred into a whirlwind of appointments. There were meetings with caterers, their tasting sessions a delightful yet stressful endeavor, a balance of culinary exploration and budget constraints. Discussions about the guest list became a delicate dance between family expectations and their personal preferences. Nikhil's extended family, a sprawling network of cousins, aunts, and uncles, added a layer of complexity, requiring careful navigation and diplomacy. Charvi's parents, while initially hesitant about the scale of the celebration, were gradually won over by their shared excitement and the meticulous planning.

The dress shopping experience was nothing short of transformative. Charvi, who'd always envisioned herself in something simple and elegant, found herself drawn to a gown far more elaborate than anticipated – a flowing silk masterpiece with intricate lace detailing, a reflection of her evolving confidence and the depth of her love for Nikhil. The moment she slipped into the dress, she felt a profound sense of self, a confident embodiment of the woman she had become. The tears that welled up weren't just tears of joy, but of gratitude for the journey that had led her to this moment. Nikhil, ever the supportive partner, was moved to silence; his eyes reflected the same awe and admiration as he witnessed her transformation.

The hunt for the perfect rings became a poignant exploration of their shared history. They opted for a minimalist design, emphasizing simplicity and sustainability, choosing recycled metals and ethically sourced stones, a conscious choice reflecting their shared environmental values. The inscription, a simple yet profound "Forever intertwined," mirrored their commitment to a journey of shared growth and unwavering support. The process itself became a reminder of their shared values and solidified their commitment to a future built on mutual understanding and respect.

Invitations, designed with recycled paper and eco-friendly inks, became another detail reflecting their personalities and values. The design, a subtle blend of rustic elegance and modern minimalism, incorporated elements of nature, reflecting their deep appreciation for the environment. The process of addressing the envelopes became a quiet, intimate ritual, a symbolic act of reaching out to the people who had shaped their lives. Each address represented a relationship, a memory, a shared experience.

Amidst the excitement and meticulous planning, a layer

of stress began to unravel. The logistical challenges of coordinating vendors, managing budgets, and addressing the myriad of details inherent in wedding planning started to take their toll. Sleepless nights became increasingly common, punctuated by frantic discussions and last-minute adjustments to the schedule. The pressure of meeting family expectations and creating a perfect day began to creep into their conversations, casting a subtle shadow over their joy.

One evening, amidst a flurry of emails and phone calls, Charvi found herself overwhelmed. The weight of the planning, the constant need to make decisions, and the fear of making mistakes proved to be more challenging than anticipated. She found herself retreating to their small apartment, feeling the familiar pangs of self-doubt creeping in. Nikhil, sensing her distress, put aside his own tasks, his work for the environmental platform momentarily forgotten. He found her curled up on the sofa, surrounded by scattered papers, her usual vibrancy dimmed.

"Tell me what's wrong," he said softly, kneeling beside her.

Charvi poured out her anxieties, the pent-up stress finally spilling over. The seemingly endless tasks, the pressure to create a "perfect" wedding, the fear of disappointing her family – it all felt overwhelming. She confessed her apprehension about the future, the uncertainties of merging two lives, two families, two distinct sets of expectations.

Nikhil listened patiently, offering not empty reassurances but empathetic understanding. He reminded her of their shared journey, their shared values, the resilience they had built together through earlier challenges. He gently pointed out the progress they had already made, the decisions they had already successfully navigated. He emphasized that the "perfect" wedding was less about perfection and more about celebrating their love, their journey, and the people who had supported them. He held her close, offering comfort and reassurance, a silent promise of unwavering support amidst the chaos.

Their response to the mounting stress wasn't to retreat, but to redefine their priorities. They created a clear division of tasks, leveraging their individual strengths to streamline the process. They consciously scheduled time for themselves, ensuring moments of peace and quiet amidst the whirlwind of activities. They sought support from their friends and family, delegating tasks and sharing the burden. They discovered that the wedding planning process wasn't just about creating a beautiful day, but about strengthening their bond, deepening their understanding, and reinforcing their commitment to each other.

The wedding preparations, initially a source of stress and uncertainty, became a testament to their resilience, their teamwork, and their unwavering love. The challenges faced and overcome strengthened their relationship, forging an even deeper connection, and proving their ability to tackle any hurdle, as long as they did so together. The wedding planning, rather than a source of conflict, became a testament to their evolving relationship – a journey of shared dreams, mutual support, and the celebration of a love story that had weathered storms and emerged stronger. The final days leading up to the wedding were a blend of controlled chaos and joyful anticipation, a beautiful culmination of months of planning and a heartfelt expression of their shared future. The impending ceremony was no longer a source of anxiety, but a celebration of their journey, a testament to their love, and a symbol of the strong bond they had forged.

Family Dynamics
Shift 🖤🖤

The aroma of cardamom and cloves hung heavy in the air, a comforting scent that usually calmed Charvi. But today, even the familiar fragrance couldn't quite soothe the nervous flutter in her stomach. Her mother, Amrita, hummed a lilting tune as she expertly pleated the silk dupatta for Charvi's mehendi ceremony, her hands moving with practiced grace. The gesture, once a source of subtle tension, now felt like a silent acknowledgment of their evolving relationship. There was a newfound ease in their interactions, a subtle shift from the initial apprehension to a tentative warmth.

Nikhil, ever the observant one, noticed the change. He'd initially felt like an outsider in the tightly knit family, a polite stranger navigating a complex web of unspoken rules and familial expectations. But over the past few months, he'd made a conscious effort to bridge the gap, engaging in conversations with Amrita and Charvi's father, Dev, about everything from cricket scores to the latest political developments. He'd learned to appreciate the subtle nuances of their communication style, understanding the underlying affection beneath the surface of their sometimes-reserved demeanor.

He watched as Dev, usually a man of few words, carefully examined the intricate design of the wedding invitation, a faint smile playing on his lips. The invitation, a collaborative effort between Charvi and Nikhil, reflected both their personalities and values—a blend of traditional aesthetics with a modern twist. It was a small detail, but it represented a significant step in bridging the generation gap. Dev, a traditionalist at heart, had initially expressed concerns about the scale of the wedding and the modern approach. Now, the subtle appreciation visible on his face spoke volumes.

"It's beautiful, Beta," Dev said, using the term of endearment reserved for those closest to his heart. The word, uttered with a warmth that surprised even Charvi, felt like a significant milestone. It was the first time he'd used it without hesitation or a hint of his initial reservations.

Later that evening, as the family gathered for dinner, the air buzzed with a comfortable energy. Conversations flowed freely, punctuated by laughter and the clinking of silverware. Nikhil's uncle, a notoriously sharp-tongued man, shared anecdotes from his own wedding, his criticisms subtly replaced with humorous observations. Charvi's aunt, initially wary of Nikhil, now regaled him with stories of her own children, a clear sign of acceptance. The table, once divided by unspoken boundaries, now felt like a gathering of friends, bound by shared joy and excitement.

The shifts weren't dramatic; they were subtle, almost imperceptible, like the gradual unfolding of a flower. It was in the shared glances, the unspoken understanding, the way Dev offered Nikhil a helping hand with the ceremonial preparations. It was in Amrita's gentle smile as she helped Charvi with her intricate henna designs, her fingers intertwining with Charvi's in a gesture of quiet affection.

One evening, Charvi found Amrita sorting through old photographs, her hands pausing on a picture of a younger Charvi, beaming at the camera. "She's grown so much,"

Amrita murmured, her voice tinged with emotion. "She's found her place in the world."

Charvi sat beside her, studying the old photographs. It struck her then, the depth of Amrita's unspoken anxieties. The wedding wasn't just about celebrating Charvi's union with Nikhil; it was also about letting go, about accepting change, and embracing the next chapter of their family's story.

Amrita's acceptance wasn't a sudden epiphany, but a gradual process of understanding, a quiet acceptance of Charvi's independence and her choice of partner.

The days leading up to the wedding were a flurry of activity, but the underlying tension had dissipated. Nikhil and Charvi actively sought to involve both families in the preparations, fostering a sense of unity and shared purpose. They delegated tasks, encouraging participation from both sides. They discovered hidden talents, rediscovered old traditions, and created new memories along the way.

Dev, who had initially been resistant to the idea of a large, elaborate wedding, enthusiastically took charge of the seating arrangements, his meticulous attention to detail ensuring everyone felt comfortable and valued. Amrita, a renowned cook, worked alongside Nikhil's mother, sharing recipes and culinary wisdom, their collaborative efforts leading to a feast that celebrated the rich heritage of both families. The siblings, initially hesitant about the large scale of the event, embraced their roles as bridesmaids and groomsmen with enthusiasm, their bonds strengthened through shared responsibilities and late-night laughter.

The wedding itself was a breathtaking culmination of months of careful planning and heartfelt efforts. It was a celebration not just of Charvi and Nikhil's love but also a testament to the resilience of family, the strength of bonds, and the transformative power of love and acceptance. The smiles on everyone's faces, especially on Dev and Amrita's, mirrored the joy and peace that had finally settled over their family. It was a celebration of new beginnings, a symbol of their shared journey, and a confirmation that even the most deeply ingrained family dynamics can shift and evolve, given time, understanding, and a whole lot of love.

The night ended with a bonfire, the flames casting dancing shadows on the faces of the assembled families. Laughter and stories filled the air, intermingling with the crackling of the fire. As Charvi and Nikhil sat side-by-side, watching the flames, they knew their journey had just begun. It was a journey of building a new home, a new life, a new family – a family that was stronger, more unified, and enriched by the very challenges they had overcome during their wedding preparations.

The wedding was not just a ceremony; it was a culmination of their journey, a symbolic representation of the evolution of their relationships, and a beacon of hope for future happiness. The intricate details of the day, from the meticulously crafted table settings to the heartfelt speeches, were interwoven with the threads of their past, present, and future, creating a tapestry rich in history, love, and the promise of what was to come. It was a reminder that even the most intricate plans can yield unexpected beauty, and that the greatest triumphs often emerge from overcoming the challenges life presents. The wedding preparations, initially a source of anxiety and uncertainty, had ultimately transformed into a catalyst for growth, strengthening their individual identities and reinforcing the bonds that held their families together. As the wedding celebrations faded into memory, what remained was the warmth of a family united, their bonds stronger than ever before. The memories of the day, etched in their hearts and minds, would serve as a constant reminder of the power of love to transform even the most complex of family dynamics.

PreWedding Jitters 🖤🖤

The day before the wedding dawned, grey and overcast, mirroring the storm brewing inside Charvi. She stared out the window of her childhood bedroom, the familiar landscape suddenly feeling alien. The vibrant hues of the wedding preparations, the bustling energy of the past few weeks, felt distant, replaced by a chilling sense of dread. It wasn't a fear of the wedding itself, not exactly. It was the weight of expectation, the unspoken anxieties, the sheer magnitude of the commitment, all coalescing into a suffocating pressure.

She picked up her phone, the image of Nikhil's smiling face her screensaver, a small comfort in the face of her mounting unease. She scrolled through their recent messages, their playful banter a stark contrast to the quiet panic squeezing her chest. A simple text – "Ready for tomorrow?" – sent a ripple of warmth through her. It wasn't a grand gesture, but it was precisely the reassurance she needed.

Later, she found herself in her quiet corner, surrounded by the wedding gifts, the delicate fabrics and intricately designed jewelry adding to the sense of overwhelming abundance. She traced the delicate embroidery on a silk shawl, a gift from her grandmother, a symbol of continuity and tradition. The weight of expectation, previously a diffuse fear, now manifested itself as a tangible pressure, the silken threads mirroring the intricate web of her anxieties. She wondered if this was what everyone felt – this pre-wedding paralysis, this unsettling mix of excitement and terror.

That evening, she found Nikhil waiting for her in the garden, a bouquet of her favorite lilies clutched in his hands. The garden, usually a vibrant explosion of colors, seemed muted under the grey sky, reflecting her inner turmoil.

"You look... pensive," he said softly, his voice a soothing balm to her frayed nerves. He sat beside her, his hand finding hers, the familiar warmth grounding her amidst the swirling emotions.

"I'm scared," she admitted, the words tumbling out in a

rush. "Scared of everything. Scared of ruining it, scared of disappointing everyone, scared of…" she trailed off, unable to articulate the nameless fears that plagued her.

Nikhil listened patiently, his eyes filled with empathy. He didn't try to minimize her feelings or offer platitudes; he simply offered his presence, his quiet support, a sanctuary amidst her storm.

"It's okay to be scared," he said gently, squeezing her hand. "It's a big day, a huge commitment. But we're doing this together. We'll face it together, whatever comes our way."

His words, simple yet profound, resonated within her, chipping away at the wall of anxiety. His presence, his unwavering support, calmed the tempest in her soul.

He shared his own anxieties, his own moments of self-doubt, revealing a vulnerability that deepened their bond. He confessed to feeling overwhelmed by the responsibility, by the weight of expectations from both families. He admitted to moments of panic, of doubting his own readiness. It was a revelation, a shared vulnerability that forged a stronger connection, reassuring her that she wasn't alone in her pre- wedding jitters.

Their conversation drifted to their shared dreams, their plans for the future, their aspirations as a couple. They talked about their hopes and fears, their excitement and apprehensions, their anxieties intertwined, yet their shared anxieties somehow lessened the individual burden. The night ended with a shared silence, a comfortable companionship that transcended words, an unspoken promise of unwavering support and shared journey.

The next morning, Charvi woke to find a hand-written note on her pillow. "You're breathtaking. I love you. Let's do this." It was simple, yet it dispelled the lingering doubts, reinforcing the certainty of her decision, the love that had brought them to this moment.

The wedding preparations continued at a frenetic pace. But this time, the chaos felt different. There was still a hum of excitement, but the undercurrent of anxiety had been replaced by a shared sense of calm, a quiet confidence born from their shared vulnerability and mutual support. They faced the challenges together, their laughter echoing in the midst of the whirlwind activity, a testament to their unwavering bond. They found themselves actively seeking moments of quiet communion, their shared silences more meaningful than any words. They held hands during the final fitting of her bridal ensemble, a shared moment of quiet reassurance amid the flurry of activity. They walked together through the garden in the quiet pre-dawn hours, finding solace in the shared space and their unspoken promises.

Charvi's mother, Amrita, noticed the change. She saw the unwavering support, the quiet moments of shared intimacy, the unspoken connection that transcended the usual pre-wedding chaos. She observed the way Nikhil anticipated Charvi's needs, the quiet empathy in his eyes, the silent reassurance in his touch. She felt a wave of relief, the anxieties she had harbored about their compatibility slowly fading away. She felt confident, not just in their marriage, but in their ability to weather any storm that life threw their way.

Dev, her father, also observed the shift, though he expressed it in his own reserved manner. He saw Nikhil engaging with his family, the effortless ease with which he interacted with his siblings, the quiet respect he showed for his elders. He observed the genuine affection that was not just expressed through words, but conveyed through subtle acts of kindness, small gestures that spoke volumes about the depth of their connection.

In the midst of the wedding preparations, amidst the flowers, the fabrics, the music, and the bustling activity, there were quiet moments of shared intimacy, moments where their eyes met and a silent understanding passed between them. It was in these quiet moments that their true bond was revealed, their shared anxieties diminished by the quiet strength of their love. They found solace in each other's company, their fears dissolving into the warmth of their love.

The wedding day arrived, bright and sunny, a stark contrast to the overcast skies of the previous day. Charvi, surrounded by her family and friends, felt a sense of calm she hadn't expected. The fear hadn't vanished entirely, but it had been replaced by a quiet confidence, a serene acceptance of the day, and the journey ahead. The jitters remained, a subtle hum beneath the surface, but they were overshadowed by the overwhelming joy, the love, and the anticipation of a future together. As she walked down the aisle, her hand in her father's, she looked into Nikhil's eyes and saw a reflection of her own calm resolve, a shared understanding that their journey, their challenges, their anxieties, had only strengthened their bond, making their love stronger, deeper, and more enduring. Their wedding was not just a celebration of their love, it was a testament to the resilience of their spirit, and a promise of a future filled with love, laughter, and the enduring strength of their shared journey.

Friends and
Celebrations 🖤🖤

The Mehndi ceremony, a vibrant explosion of color and tradition, unfolded in the sprawling backyard of Charvi's family home. The air thrummed with the rhythmic beat of dhol drums, a hypnotic pulse that set the celebratory mood. The scent of henna, earthy and intoxicating, mingled with the aroma of delicious street food – pav bhaji, chaat, and samosas – laid out on brightly colored tablecloths. Laughter spilled from every corner, a joyous cacophony that resonated with the swirling energy of the event. Charvi, her hands adorned with intricate henna patterns, found herself at the heart of it all, surrounded by her closest friends. Their laughter, their teasing, their shared secrets, were a comforting balm, a reassuring reminder of the enduring strength of their friendship. They reminisced about childhood adventures, silly teenage escapades, and the shared milestones that had shaped their lives. Each shared story, each inside joke, was a testament to their enduring bond, a source of strength and comfort amidst the wedding chaos. Priya, her best friend since kindergarten, dabbed a stray henna stain from Charvi's cheek, her eyes reflecting a mixture of happiness and a hint of bittersweet nostalgia. "Can't believe you're actually getting married," she said, her voice choked with emotion. "It feels like yesterday we were sneaking out to see Bollywood movies." The others echoed her sentiments, each sharing a personal anecdote, a cherished memory, their collective voice weaving a tapestry of laughter, tears, and shared history. They danced together, their movements clumsy yet joyful, their laughter echoing through the garden. It was a celebration not just of Charvi's impending marriage but also of their enduring friendship, a bond that had stood the test of time, a testament to their shared journey.

The Sangeet night, a kaleidoscope of music and dance, offered a different kind of celebration. This was a fusion of families, a blending of cultures, a vibrant tapestry woven from the individual threads of two families coming together. The stage, bathed in the soft glow of colorful lights, transformed into a canvas for the expressions of love, joy, and shared memories. Family members, friends, and even some distant relatives, took turns performing dances, each performance imbued with individual meaning and emotion. Charvi's aunts and cousins, dressed in dazzling sarees, performed a traditional Garba dance, their graceful movements echoing generations of tradition. Nikhil's uncles and cousins, in their dapper kurtas, responded with a high- energy Bhangra, their infectious energy captivating the audience. The music, a vibrant blend of traditional Indian melodies and contemporary Bollywood beats, filled the air, urging everyone onto the dance floor. Charvi and Nikhil, taking the stage together, performed a romantic dance, their movements reflecting the depth of their love, their eyes locking in shared moments of unspoken affection. The atmosphere was electric, filled with a palpable sense of joy and unity, a celebration of two families embracing each other, their hearts interwoven in the rhythm of the music and dance. It was a celebration of coming together, of shared traditions, of building a new family, united by love and mutual respect.

The following day, a relaxed brunch at a scenic vineyard offered a quieter, more intimate celebration. This gathering brought together a smaller group – Charvi and Nikhil's closest friends and family members – creating an atmosphere of relaxed intimacy. The setting, picturesque and serene, provided the perfect backdrop for meaningful conversations and laughter-filled reminiscences. The food, gourmet and delicious, complemented the elegant ambiance. The conversations were relaxed, laughter filled the air, and the bond between the guests was palpable. The discussions ranged from childhood memories to dreams for the future, creating a warm and meaningful setting. It was a time for shared stories, inside jokes, and the creation of new memories. Each conversation strengthened the bonds between individuals, creating a unique sense of community, a comforting feeling of being surrounded by love and support. It was a moment of reflection and gratitude, a chance to appreciate the people who played a significant role in shaping Charvi and Nikhil's lives. It was in this intimate setting that the true strength of their relationships became apparent, the bonds of friendship and family, strengthened by time and shared experiences.

The bridal shower, held at a friend's charming cottage, offered a different kind of celebration – a playful blend of pampering and heartfelt wishes. The setting, warm and cozy, felt like a comforting embrace, creating a haven of laughter and friendship. The girls showered Charvi with gifts, thoughtful presents that represented their affection and support. It wasn't just about the presents, though; it was the heartfelt wishes, the shared stories, the laughter, and the collective feeling of love and support that made the bridal shower so special. There were games, of course – silly games that tested their knowledge of Charvi and Nikhil's relationship, igniting laughter and playful banter. There were heartfelt speeches, moments of genuine emotion that brought tears to some eyes and warmth to everyone's hearts. The afternoon unfolded as a gentle tapestry of love, laughter, and shared experiences, creating a lasting memory of friendship and togetherness. The celebration was intimate and heartwarming, leaving Charvi with a sense of deep gratitude for the support and love surrounding her.

As the wedding day approached, a sense of shared anticipation permeated every gathering, every conversation, every interaction. The celebrations were not just about the wedding itself; they were about the people who had played a significant role in shaping Charvi and Nikhil's lives, about the bonds of friendship and family that had strengthened over time, about the shared journey that had led them to this momentous occasion. The joyous energy of the celebrations, the shared laughter and tears, the heartfelt wishes, and the expressions of love and support, all served to create a tapestry of unforgettable memories. These celebrations were a prelude to the wedding, a fitting testament to the love and support that surrounded the couple, a heartfelt affirmation of the enduring strength of human connection. They were the building blocks of a future together, each celebration a step closer to the new chapter they were about to embark on.

Each celebration was a testament to the power of love, friendship, and family, shaping their journey, strengthening their bond, and setting the stage for their happily ever after. The whirlwind of preparations, the vibrant tapestry of emotions, and the joyous celebrations all blended together, forming a beautiful prelude to the wedding day itself. And as the day drew nearer, a sense of anticipation, of excitement, of shared joy, filled the air, promising a celebration that would transcend the usual wedding fanfare, a celebration that would resonate long after the last dance and the final farewell.

The Wedding Eve 💕

The air hung heavy with unspoken emotions, a quiet hum beneath the surface of the usual pre-wedding bustle. Charvi sat on the plush, cream-colored carpet of her childhood bedroom, surrounded by a chaotic yet comforting array of silken sarees, glittering jewelry, and half-packed suitcases. The room, usually a haven of youthful energy and strewn with books and sketches, was transformed into a meticulously organized space, a testament to the meticulous efforts of her family. But the organized chaos couldn't mask the underlying current of emotion. This wasn't just any night; it was the eve of her wedding.

Her mother, ever the picture of calm amidst the storm, bustled about, her fingers deftly arranging the folds of a shimmering gold saree. Her father, usually reserved, sat on the edge of the bed, a half-finished cup of chai resting on the bedside table, his eyes reflecting a mixture of pride and a hint of melancholy. He cleared his throat, his gaze lingering on Charvi. "You know," he began, his voice raspy with emotion, "it feels like just yesterday you were a little girl, scrabbling in the garden for earthworms." A faint smile touched his lips. "And now, look at you."

His words triggered a cascade of memories. Charvi remembered her father's patient hand guiding hers as she learned to ride a bicycle, the shared laughter during family movie nights, the countless stories he'd told her before bedtime. The memories, both poignant and joyful, brought a lump to her throat. She reached out and took her father's hand, her own trembling slightly. "I love you, Papa," she whispered, the words brimming with gratitude.

Her mother joined them, her eyes shining with unshed tears. "My little girl is all grown up," she murmured, her voice thick with emotion. She wrapped Charvi in a warm embrace, the scent of her familiar perfume – a blend of jasmine and sandalwood – a comforting balm. It was a silent communion of love and acceptance, a shared moment of unspoken understanding.

Priya, her best friend, arrived shortly after, bringing with her a basket overflowing with snacks and a bottle of chilled champagne. The sight of Priya, her face illuminated by the warm glow of the lamplight, brought an immediate sense of relief and familiarity. "Relax," Priya said, her voice brisk yet gentle. "You've planned this wedding down to the last detail. Now, it's time to let go and enjoy the moment."

They spent the next few hours reminiscing, sharing stories and secrets, their laughter echoing through the room. Priya recounted their escapades – the time they dyed their principal's hair blue, the hilarious attempt at baking a cake that ended in a kitchen catastrophe, and their countless late- night talks about dreams, fears, and everything in between.

Each story was a precious gem, a testament to their unbreakable bond, a source of strength and comfort in the midst of the wedding frenzy.

As the night deepened, the intensity of the emotions shifted. The playful banter gave way to more reflective conversations, a tender exploration of the journey that had led them to this point. They talked about Nikhil, his kindness, his gentle humor, his unwavering support. They talked about the challenges they had faced, the obstacles they had overcome, the shared dreams they were about to embark upon. There was a palpable sense of appreciation, a shared gratitude for the journey, for the experiences that had shaped them, for the love that bound them together.

Later, as the city outside slumbered, Charvi found herself alone in the room, surrounded by the quiet hush of the night. The wedding preparations were complete; the last of the errands run, the last of the calls made. The sense of anticipation was immense, but it was interwoven with a sense of peace, a quiet confidence in her choice, in her future. She looked out of the window at the moonlit cityscape, a myriad of lights twinkling like distant stars. It was a breathtaking sight, a silent backdrop to her own internal reflection.

She thought of Nikhil, his gentle smile, his reassuring touch, his unwavering faith in their future. The love they shared was a beacon of hope, a guiding light amidst the uncertainty of the unknown. She visualized their life together, the joys, the challenges, the shared journey that lay ahead. It was a mixture of excitement and trepidation, a leap of faith into the vast expanse of their future.

In the quiet solitude, a feeling of gratitude washed over her. She was grateful for her family, for their unwavering support, their endless love. She was grateful for her friends, for their laughter, their encouragement, their unconditional friendship. And she was profoundly grateful for Nikhil, for his love, his trust, and his unwavering belief in their love story. The wedding was not just a celebration of their union, it was a celebration of their individual journeys, a culmination of their shared experiences, a testament to the power of love and connection. It was the beginning of a new chapter, a new adventure, a journey of shared dreams and aspirations, a life spent together.

The stillness of the night was broken only by the distant sounds of the city, a gentle lullaby as Charvi drifted off to sleep, her heart filled with a mixture of excitement, anticipation, and a profound sense of peace. It was the eve of her wedding, a significant milestone, a culmination of a lifelong journey, a promise of a future filled with shared dreams and limitless possibilities. The wedding was not just a celebration of love; it was a celebration of life, a celebration of connection, a celebration of the enduring power of human bonds. It was the perfect ending to one chapter and the exhilarating beginning of another. The next morning would be a day of joy, a day of celebration, a day of new beginnings. But tonight, in the quiet solitude of her childhood bedroom, she savored the quietude, the anticipation, the profound sense of peace that enveloped her like a warm embrace. It was a night of reflection, a night of gratitude, a night of dreams. And as she fell asleep, she knew that the adventure was just beginning.

The Wedding Day ♥♥

The morning sun streamed through the sheer curtains of Charvi's room, painting the walls in a soft, golden hue. It was a day unlike any other, a day brimming with anticipation, a day that held the promise of forever. The air buzzed with a frenetic energy, a symphony of activity orchestrated by her family and friends. The familiar scent of jasmine and sandalwood, her mother's signature perfume, hung faintly in the air, a comforting reminder of home, of family, of love.

The meticulously planned schedule unfolded with a gentle grace. The sounds of bustling activity filtered through the closed door – the soft murmur of voices, the rhythmic clinking of silverware, the gentle hum of the air conditioning. It was a carefully choreographed dance of preparation, a ballet of efficiency and love. But amidst the controlled chaos, there was a palpable sense of peace, a calm that emanated from Charvi herself. She felt an overwhelming sense of gratitude, a deep appreciation for the journey that had led her to this moment.

Her wedding saree, a masterpiece of shimmering ivory silk, lay draped over a plush velvet chair, its intricate embroidery catching the light like a thousand tiny stars. The delicate jewelry, passed down through generations, rested on a satin cushion, each piece a testament to family history, a tangible link to the past. As she slipped into the saree, the cool silk against her skin felt like a calming embrace, a soothing antidote to the fluttering in her heart. Her mother helped her with the intricate pleats and drapes, her deft fingers moving with practiced ease. It was a silent ritual, a tender exchange of unspoken words, a shared moment of quiet joy.

The makeup artist, a skilled professional, worked her magic, transforming Charvi into a radiant bride. Each stroke of the brush, each application of color, was a delicate touch, enhancing her natural beauty without masking her essence. As she gazed at her reflection, Charvi saw not just a beautiful bride, but a woman transformed, a woman filled with love, hope, and anticipation. The years of growth, the struggles, the joys – all had converged to this point, shaping her into the woman she was now, ready to embark on a new adventure.

The journey to the wedding venue was a blur of emotions. The car ride felt like a dream, a surreal experience, the cityscape swirling past in a kaleidoscope of colors. Her father sat beside her, his hand gently resting on hers, his silence a comforting presence. He didn't need words; his presence was enough, a testament to his unwavering love and support. It was a shared silence, a profound understanding between father and daughter, a moment that transcended words.

The wedding venue was a breathtaking spectacle, a haven of elegance and charm. The air was filled with the intoxicating scent of flowers, a fragrant tapestry of roses, lilies, and jasmine. Soft music played in the background, setting a tranquil and romantic mood. As Charvi stepped out of the car, a collective gasp of admiration rippled through the gathered guests. She was a vision, a radiant bride bathed in the soft glow of the setting sun.

The ceremony unfolded like a sacred ritual, a beautiful blend of tradition and modernity. The familiar chants and prayers, the exchange of vows, the sacred rituals – each moment felt deeply personal, deeply meaningful. Nikhil, her groom, stood before her, his eyes sparkling with love and admiration. As she looked into his eyes, she saw not just her future husband, but her best friend, her confidante, her soulmate. It was a moment of profound connection, a shared understanding that transcended words.

Their vows, spoken with heartfelt sincerity, echoed through the venue, a testament to their love, their commitment, their shared dreams. They promised to love, honor, and cherish each other, through thick and thin, through joy and sorrow, through the challenges and triumphs of life. Their vows were not just promises; they were a sacred pact, a commitment to a lifetime of shared adventures.

The ceremony concluded with a shower of rose petals, a symbolic blessing, a shower of love and happiness. As they stood hand-in-hand, surrounded by their loved ones, Charvi felt a wave of overwhelming emotion. It was a moment of pure joy, a moment of profound gratitude, a moment that encapsulated everything she had ever dreamed of.

The reception was a vibrant celebration, a kaleidoscope of laughter, music, and dance. Friends and family mingled, sharing stories and memories, their joy infectious. The air was filled with laughter, the music pulsated with energy, and the dance floor was alive with movement. It was a night of unrestrained joy, a testament to the love and happiness that enveloped them.

The first dance, a slow, graceful waltz, was a private moment, a shared intimacy amidst the celebratory chaos. As they swayed to the music, Charvi felt Nikhil's hand in hers, a comforting presence, a reassuring touch. It was a moment of silent communion, a shared acknowledgment of their journey, a testament to the love that bound them together.

As the night deepened, the energy shifted, the vibrant celebration giving way to a more intimate gathering. Close friends and family gathered, sharing stories and memories, their laughter echoing through the night. It was a time of reflection, a shared acknowledgment of the journey that had led them to this point.

The night culminated in a breathtaking display of fireworks, illuminating the night sky with a thousand shimmering stars. It was a symbolic ending to the day, a dazzling display of love, happiness, and hope. As the fireworks faded, Charvi and Nikhil stood hand-in-hand, gazing at the night sky, their hearts filled with a mixture of joy, gratitude, and anticipation.

The wedding day was more than just a celebration; it was a culmination, a testament to their love story, a promise of forever. It was a day filled with emotions – joy, love, happiness, gratitude – a day that would forever be etched in their memories. As they drove away from the venue, hand in hand, Charvi knew that their adventure had just begun, a new chapter, a new journey, a life spent together. The city lights twinkled, mirroring the sparkling joy in their hearts, a promise of a future filled with love, laughter, and limitless possibilities. The journey had been long, but it had led them to this perfect moment, a moment of pure, unadulterated joy, a beginning to their forever after. And as they drove into the night, the city lights a backdrop to their happiness, Charvi knew, with unwavering certainty, that this was just the beginning of their happily ever after.

Married Life Begins 🖤

The car pulled up to their new home, a charming little bungalow nestled in a quiet suburban neighborhood. It wasn't grand, not like the opulent venues of their wedding, but it felt perfectly theirs. As Charvi stepped out, Nikhil took her hand, his touch sending a familiar warmth through her. The air hummed with a different kind of energy now, not the frenetic pace of the wedding day, but a quiet, intimate buzz of anticipation. This was their space, their haven, the foundation of their forever.

The house was filled with the fresh scent of paint and new beginnings. Sunlight streamed through the large windows, illuminating the airy rooms, still echoing with the faint scent of unpacking. Boxes lay scattered about, a testament to the ongoing process of settling in, but amidst the organized chaos, there was a palpable sense of home. They'd spent weeks choosing paint colors, furniture, and decor, carefully crafting a space that reflected their shared tastes and personalities. Each item felt imbued with a piece of their story, a shared memory, a promise of a life lived together.

The first few days were a whirlwind of unpacking, organizing, and navigating the simple joys and challenges of daily life. They laughed over mismatched socks, argued playfully over whose turn it was to do the dishes, and shared quiet moments curled up on the sofa, lost in the world of their favorite TV shows. It was a period of adjustment, a subtle shift from the individual lives they once led to the shared rhythm of a married couple. It wasn't always easy; there were moments of frustration, of misunderstanding, but those moments only served to strengthen their bond, to deepen their understanding of each other.

Evenings were spent exploring their neighborhood, hand-in- hand, discovering local gems—a cozy bookstore, a hidden café with the best coffee, a park where they could spend hours just talking, sharing dreams, and making plans for the future. Simple meals cooked together, punctuated by laughter and shared stories, became a cherished ritual. The clinking of forks and knives against plates, the soft murmur of conversations, created a symphony of intimacy, a comforting backdrop to their shared life.

Charvi found herself waking up each morning with a smile on her face. The mundane tasks – making coffee, preparing breakfast, folding laundry – had a newfound meaning, infused with a subtle sweetness, a sense of purpose that came from sharing them with Nikhil. It wasn't the grand gestures of romance that defined their days, but the small, quiet moments, the shared smiles, the gentle touches, the unspoken understanding that grew with each passing day.

Nikhil, usually so focused on his work, found himself craving these quiet moments even more. The pressures of his career, once an all-consuming force, seemed to melt away in the warmth of their shared home. He discovered a new kind of fulfillment, a deeper sense of contentment that stemmed from the love and companionship he found in Charvi. The daily routine, once a predictable cycle, now held a sense of wonder, a constant reminder of the beautiful life they were building together.

One evening, while curled up on the sofa, lost in the pages of their favorite book, Nikhil gently brushed a stray strand of hair from Charvi's face. Their eyes met, a silent exchange of unspoken words, a profound understanding that transcended any need for articulation. In that moment, surrounded by the quiet intimacy of their home, they found a peace they had never known before. It was a comfortable silence, a shared contentment that spoke volumes more than any words could express.

Their weekends were filled with exploring their newfound city. They discovered hidden cafes tucked away in quiet alleyways, antique shops filled with treasures from the past, and parks where they could spend lazy afternoons, just talking, dreaming, and making plans for the future. They attended local art fairs, marveling at the creativity and talent displayed, and shared evenings in front of a crackling fireplace, their laughter echoing through the cozy space.

Their relationship, once defined by grand gestures and romantic encounters, found a deeper meaning in these simple, shared experiences.

They also faced minor challenges. Nikhil's habit of leaving his socks scattered around the house clashed with Charvi's meticulous organization. There were occasional disagreements over household chores, minor arguments that served to clarify their individual needs and preferences. But these moments, rather than weakening their bond, only seemed to strengthen it, teaching them the importance of communication, compromise, and understanding.

Slowly, their house began to feel less like a collection of boxes and furniture and more like a true home, reflecting their personalities and their evolving relationship.

Photographs from their wedding day adorned the walls, a constant reminder of their commitment and the love that bound them. Small, meaningful gifts – a hand-painted mug, a framed photograph from their travels, a small potted plant – added touches of personal style and affection. Each object held a story, a memory, a piece of their shared journey.

One Sunday afternoon, they decided to cook a meal together, their aprons a testament to their evolving domestic lives. The flour dusted their clothes, their laughter filled the air, and their shared efforts resulted in a delicious pasta dish that far exceeded their culinary expectations. It wasn't simply a meal; it was an experience shared, a moment of creation, a symbol of their growing partnership.

As the weeks turned into months, Charvi and Nikhil settled into a comfortable rhythm, a dance of shared responsibilities and unspoken understanding. They discovered the beauty of ordinary days, the quiet joys that came with creating a life together. Their laughter echoed through their home, their quiet moments of intimacy woven into the tapestry of their everyday lives. Theirs wasn't a fairy-tale romance; it was a genuine, relatable love story, built on respect, understanding, and the shared commitment to a future filled with love, laughter, and shared adventures.

One evening, while sitting on their porch, watching the sunset paint the sky in hues of orange and pink, Charvi leaned her head against Nikhil's shoulder. The silence between them was comfortable, a shared understanding that needed no words. In that moment, she felt a profound sense of contentment, a deep appreciation for the life they had created together. It was a life of quiet moments and shared dreams, a life built on a foundation of love, trust, and unwavering commitment. This was their forever after, not a magical fairy tale, but a real-life story of love, resilience, and the joy of finding your soulmate in the most ordinary of days. The journey had only just begun, but they were in it together, hand-in-hand, ready to face whatever life threw their way, their love a constant and unwavering compass guiding their path. The future stretched ahead, an uncharted territory filled with possibilities, but with each other by their side, they knew they could face anything. Their forever after was not a destination but a journey, a shared adventure filled with love, laughter, and the quiet comfort of home.

Challenges and
Growth 🖤💜

The first real test came unexpectedly, in the form of Nikhil's grandmother, Dadi. Dadi, a formidable woman with a heart of gold and opinions as strong as her chai, had always been a significant presence in Nikhil's life. Her arrival for an extended visit, initially intended as a joyful family reunion, soon turned into a subtle source of tension. Dadi, steeped in traditional values, had a distinct way of doing things, a way that clashed occasionally with Charvi's more modern approach to housekeeping and daily life.

Small disagreements escalated into larger conflicts. Dadi's preference for a particular type of rice, meticulously sourced from her village, clashed with Charvi's attempts to introduce healthier, more convenient options. The way they organized the kitchen became a battleground, each woman defending her territory with gentle but firm conviction. Charvi, used to her own independent lifestyle, found herself grappling with a loss of control, a feeling of being constantly scrutinized.

Nikhil, caught between his wife and his grandmother, felt the weight of mediating their differences, a role he wasn't entirely comfortable with.

One evening, after a particularly tense dinner, a heated argument erupted. Charvi, feeling unheard and overwhelmed, retreated to their bedroom, leaving Nikhil to smooth things over with his grandmother. The air in the house felt thick with unspoken resentments. That night, Nikhil found Charvi curled up in bed, tears silently tracing paths down her cheeks. He sat beside her, gently stroking her hair, and listened patiently as she poured out her frustrations, her fears of not measuring up to Dadi's expectations, of not being the perfect granddaughter-in-law.

Nikhil's heart ached for her. He understood her feelings, the subtle pressure of conforming to family expectations, the silent battle to maintain her individuality while navigating a new family dynamic. He reassured her, reminding her of their shared values, their love for each other, and the strength of their bond. He acknowledged her feelings, validated her frustrations, and promised to be her advocate. He gently explained Dadi's perspective, her deep-rooted attachment to traditions, her underlying love and concern.

The next day, Nikhil intervened, initiating a conversation with his grandmother. He carefully explained Charvi's perspective, emphasizing their mutual respect and love, and highlighting their shared desire to honor family traditions while creating their own unique family dynamic. Dadi, initially resistant, began to understand. She saw the depth of their love, the strength of their commitment. A compromise was reached, a delicate balance between tradition and modernity, between Dadi's expectations and Charvi's individuality. The tension eased, replaced by a newfound understanding and appreciation for each other.

The challenges didn't end with Dadi's visit. Nikhil's demanding career continued to present hurdles. Late nights at the office, stressful deadlines, and the ever-present pressure to succeed created a strain on their relationship.

Charvi, worried about his well-being, expressed her concerns. She didn't want to be a burden, but she also longed for more of his time, more moments of shared intimacy. The discussions weren't always easy; they involved compromises, adjustments, and a willingness to understand each other's perspectives.

One particular evening, Nikhil missed their anniversary dinner due to a last-minute work crisis. The disappointment was palpable. Charvi's initial reaction was hurt, a feeling of being overlooked and undervalued. But instead of letting resentment fester, she chose to communicate her feelings openly and honestly. Nikhil, equally hurt by his missed opportunity to celebrate their love, apologized profusely, expressing his regret and his deep love for her. He showed his remorse not just with words but with actions – a special surprise breakfast the next morning, a heartfelt handwritten letter expressing his love and appreciation, a spontaneous weekend getaway to a cozy cabin in the woods. The missed anniversary became a turning point, a reminder that even the most challenging circumstances couldn't diminish the strength of their bond. It taught them the importance of open communication, of empathy, and the power of forgiveness.

Their struggles weren't confined to personal issues. They encountered financial challenges, unexpected home repairs, and the stress of navigating the complexities of adult life. These trials, though seemingly insurmountable at times, only served to strengthen their resolve, to deepen their understanding of each other's strengths and weaknesses. They learned to lean on each other, to share responsibilities, and to find solutions together. They discovered that their love wasn't just a romantic ideal but a practical partnership, a source of strength and resilience in the face of adversity.

Through it all, their home remained their sanctuary, a haven where they could retreat from the storms of life and find solace in each other's arms. The walls, once adorned with wedding photographs, now showcased pictures of their shared experiences – a hike in the mountains, a picnic in the park, a quiet evening spent reading together. Each photograph was a testament to their journey, a reminder of their growth, and their enduring love. The house wasn't just a building; it was a living, breathing testament to their evolving relationship, a symbol of their commitment, resilience, and unwavering love.

Their love story wasn't a fairy tale, devoid of conflict or challenge. It was a realistic portrayal of a relationship in its truest form – messy, complicated, and sometimes painful, yet ultimately filled with love, laughter, and unwavering commitment. The challenges they faced weren't obstacles to overcome, but opportunities to grow, to learn, and to deepen their bond. Their journey taught them that "forever after" wasn't a destination, but a continuous process of learning, adapting, and growing together, hand-in-hand, through the trials and triumphs of life. Their love was not a fleeting emotion but a foundation, a solid bedrock upon which they built their life, their home, and their forever. The journey was far from over, yet they were ready, together, to face whatever the future held, their love their guiding star. Their story wasn't just about a wedding, but about the ongoing commitment, the unwavering support, and the unwavering belief in the power of love to conquer all. The sunsets they watched together, the quiet moments shared over a cup of coffee, the laughter that echoed through their home—these were the true building blocks of their forever after. And as they navigated the complexities of their life together, they knew that their journey, their forever, was the most beautiful story they would ever write.

Celebrating

Milestones 🖤🖤

Their first anniversary was a quiet affair, a stark contrast to the grand wedding celebration. They opted for a cozy dinner at home, candlelight flickering on the table, illuminating the soft glow on Charvi's face as she laughed at one of Nikhil's stories. It wasn't about extravagance; it was about intimacy, a quiet celebration of the year they'd spent building a life together. Nikhil presented her with a delicate silver necklace, a simple pendant shaped like a tiny intertwined heart, a symbol of their enduring bond. That night, as they lay nestled in bed, they reminisced about their journey, the challenges overcome, and the unwavering love that had seen them through. The quiet intimacy of the evening cemented the foundation of their "forever after," a testament to their shared journey.

Their second anniversary saw them embark on a

spontaneous road trip. With packed bags and a playlist of their favorite songs, they drove along the coast, the wind whipping through their hair, their laughter echoing in the car. They stopped at quaint roadside diners, savored ice cream on the beach, and watched sunsets paint the sky with breathtaking hues. The journey itself became a metaphor for their relationship – a winding road with unexpected turns, but always leading them closer to each other. The memories created during that road trip were as vivid and vibrant as the landscapes they traversed, each moment a treasured memory woven into the tapestry of their love story.

The holidays brought a different kind of celebration. Diwali, with its dazzling lights and vibrant festivities, became a canvas for their shared traditions. They lit diyas, exchanged sweets, and enjoyed the joyous atmosphere with family and friends. Christmas, with its cozy warmth and festive cheer, saw them decorating their home with twinkling lights and exchanging heartfelt gifts. These occasions weren't just about celebrating the holidays; they were about creating shared traditions, weaving their individual histories into a beautiful tapestry of shared experiences. Each festivity was a reminder of their evolving identity as a couple, a testament to the love that blossomed amidst the celebrations.

Then came the birth of their first child, a momentous occasion that redefined their "forever after." The arrival of their little one brought with it a wave of profound joy, mingled with the overwhelming responsibility of parenthood. The sleepless nights, the endless diaper changes, and the constant worry were overshadowed by the sheer, unconditional love they felt for their child. Their roles shifted, but their love remained the steady anchor amidst the changing tides of parenthood. Their home, once a sanctuary for just the two of them, now resonated with the sweet sounds of baby giggles, transforming into a haven of love and family. The addition of their child painted a new chapter in their love story, a testament to the enduring strength of their bond.

The years that followed were filled with both triumphs and tribulations. Nikhil's career continued to present challenges, requiring long hours and demanding travel. Charvi pursued her own ambitions, juggling her work with the responsibilities of motherhood. They navigated the complexities of work-life balance, learning to lean on each other, to share responsibilities, and to prioritize their family. Their communication remained open and honest, their love a constant source of support and encouragement. Through it all, their home remained their anchor, a place where they could reconnect, recharge, and celebrate their love amidst the chaos of life.

One particularly memorable anniversary saw them return to the place where they first met, a small café tucked away on a quiet street. Sitting at the same table, they reminisced about their first encounter, the nervous laughter, the shy smiles, and the spark that ignited their love. The years had passed, but the warmth and affection they felt for each other remained as vibrant as ever. It was a reminder of how far they'd come, the journey they'd shared, and the enduring strength of their love. The café, once a symbol of a burgeoning romance, had now become a testament to their enduring love story.

Another milestone was their fifth anniversary, a celebration of five years of shared laughter, tears, and unwavering commitment. They renewed their vows in a small, intimate ceremony, surrounded by close friends and family. The simplicity of the occasion was a reflection of their evolving relationship, a testament to the enduring love that had stood the test of time. Their renewed vows weren't just words; they were a reaffirmation of their commitment, a promise to continue their journey together, hand in hand, through whatever life threw their way. The quiet solemnity of the moment underscored the depth of their commitment, a promise silently exchanged, a vow renewed, and a future envisioned together.

Over the years, their home became a living testament to their love story. The walls were adorned not just with wedding photos, but with cherished memories – pictures of family vacations, school plays, sporting events, and casual moments captured at home. Each photograph was a snapshot of their life together, a reminder of their growth, and their enduring love. Their home was not just a place to live; it was a living, breathing chronicle of their shared life, a testament to the strength of their bond.

Their tenth anniversary was a grand celebration, a recognition of a decade spent building a life together, weathering storms, and celebrating triumphs. They threw a lavish party, inviting friends and family to join them in celebrating their enduring love. The night was filled with laughter, dancing, and heartfelt speeches, a testament to the depth of their relationships and the enduring strength of their love. The grand celebration wasn't just about marking a decade; it was a celebration of their shared journey, a testament to their resilience, and a promise of many more years of love and happiness together.

Throughout their journey, their communication remained the cornerstone of their relationship. They learned to express their feelings openly and honestly, to listen empathetically, and to find solutions together. Disagreements arose, but they learned to navigate them with patience, understanding, and unwavering love. Their communication wasn't always easy; it required compromise, adjustment, and a willingness to understand each other's perspectives. However, their commitment to open communication became their strength, their unwavering love their guiding light.

Their love story wasn't a fairytale; it was a realistic portrayal of a relationship in its truest form – messy, complicated, and sometimes painful, yet ultimately filled with love, laughter, and unwavering commitment. The challenges they faced were not obstacles to overcome, but opportunities to grow, to learn, and to deepen their bond. Their journey taught them that "forever after" wasn't a destination, but a continuous process of learning, adapting, and growing together, hand in hand, through the trials and triumphs of life. Their love was not a fleeting emotion but a foundation, a solid bedrock upon which they built their life, their home, and their forever. The sunsets they watched together, the quiet moments shared over a cup of coffee, the laughter that echoed through their home – these were the true building blocks of their forever after. And as they navigated the complexities of their life together, they knew that their journey, their forever, was the most beautiful story they would ever write.

Looking to the Future 💕

The sun streamed through the kitchen window, painting stripes of gold across the worn wooden floor. Charvi hummed a tuneless melody, her fingers deftly kneading dough for their favorite cinnamon rolls. The aroma of baking bread, a comforting constant in their home, filled the air, a fragrant testament to the years they'd spent building their life together. Nikhil, his face illuminated by the morning light, sat at the kitchen table, engrossed in a book, the gentle rustle of pages providing a peaceful counterpoint to Charvi's humming. Their daughter, now a teenager, was upstairs, lost in the world of online homework and teenage anxieties. Life, as it always had been, was a symphony of moments, both quiet and vibrant, all woven into the rich tapestry of their shared existence.

Their future wasn't a meticulously planned itinerary; it was a canvas of possibilities, a space where dreams could take flight and aspirations could blossom. Nikhil dreamt of expanding his work, his passion for his field leading him to mentor aspiring young entrepreneurs. The thought filled him with a sense of purpose, of giving back to a world that had been so kind to him. He envisioned workshops, conferences, maybe even writing a book to share his knowledge and experience. The idea wasn't just about professional advancement, it was about creating a legacy, leaving a positive impact, and inspiring others to achieve their own dreams.

Charvi, meanwhile, harbored her own aspirations. She planned to take a class in pottery, a skill that had always intrigued her. The idea of working with clay, the feel of it between her fingers, held a deep-seated appeal; it represented a path toward self-expression, a journey of artistic exploration, away from the stresses of work and everyday life. The pottery classes were more than a hobby; they were a chance to reconnect with a part of herself, to indulge in creativity, and to unleash a side of her that had remained dormant for too long. Beyond pottery, she longed to travel more with Nikhil and their daughter, to explore new countries, and immerse themselves in different cultures. The opportunity to see the world through their eyes held immense appeal for her.

Their daughter, amidst her teenage turmoil and academic pressures, was starting to forge her own path. They encouraged her passions, nurturing her artistic inclinations, and supporting her every step of the way. They were committed to providing her with the freedom to explore her own identity, to discover her dreams, and to navigate the complexities of adolescence with grace. Their role as parents evolved alongside their child's growth, the transition being a testament to the adaptability and love within their family.

Their future wasn't about grand gestures or dramatic turns of events; it was about the quiet joys of everyday life – the shared cups of coffee in the morning, the laughter that filled their home, the late-night conversations whispered under the covers, the quiet understanding that existed between them without words being spoken. It was about continuing to grow together, to learn from each other, to support each other's dreams.

They envisioned family vacations, filled with laughter,

shared experiences, and countless memories to cherish. They pictured themselves exploring hidden corners of the world, capturing moments of wonder through photographs, and sharing those experiences with their loved ones. The future wasn't solely about them; it included extended family and cherished friends. Their relationship had always been about inclusivity, welcoming others into their circle and sharing the joy of their life. Their extended family and friends were woven into their fabric.

Their conversations, always a cornerstone of their relationship, would remain a vital component of their shared future. They would continue to share their joys, sorrows, hopes and fears. Their commitment to open communication was the bedrock upon which their relationship was built. It was an understanding that enabled them to navigate the ever- changing landscapes of their lives together. They envisioned continuing to support each other's dreams, providing encouragement and guidance.

Financial stability was also a part of their future plans, not for material gain but for the peace of mind it offered. They aimed to create a secure financial footing for themselves and their daughter, ensuring her future prospects and their overall stability. This wasn't about wealth; it was about security, providing a solid foundation for their family to flourish.

Their home, a testament to their shared life, would remain a constant. It wasn't just a house; it was a haven, a place of refuge, comfort, and immense love. They would continue to fill it with memories, photographs, and countless moments etched in the fabric of their shared lives. They visualized their home filled with joy, warmth, and the comforting sounds of a family united in love.

Their future wasn't devoid of challenges. Life, in its unpredictable nature, would inevitably present its share of difficulties. But they were prepared. Their relationship was built on a foundation of mutual respect, unwavering love, and a commitment to weathering any storm. They knew that the storms would come, but they would face them together, their bond an anchor amidst the turbulence.

Their faith in themselves, in each other, and in their shared future remained steadfast. Their optimistic outlook was not naive; it was a belief in their resilience, in their ability to overcome adversity, and in the enduring power of their love. They knew that life was a journey, not a destination. And they were ready to embrace every twist and turn of that journey, hand in hand, their love a guiding light.

Their "forever after" wasn't a fairytale ending; it was the ongoing story of a love that deepened with each passing year. It was a testament to the power of shared dreams, unwavering commitment, and an enduring love that transcended time and circumstance. It was the simple joys, the quiet moments, the shared laughter, and the quiet understanding that would continue to define their journey. As they looked towards their future, they saw not a destination but a horizon brimming with possibilities, a canvas awaiting the strokes of their shared journey, a testament to a love that would continue to grow and flourish, year after year, creating a beautiful masterpiece of "forever after". And in those quiet moments, shared over a cup of coffee or a warm embrace, they found the beauty and the truth in their enduring love, a love that whispered promises of a lifetime of happiness, a testament to their "forever after." The sun set on another day, painting the sky in hues of orange and purple, mirroring the warmth and vibrancy of their love. And as they stood side-by-side, hand in hand, they knew that their story, their "forever after," was just beginning.

Acknowledgments

First and foremost, I want to express my deepest gratitude to my family and friends, whose unwavering support and belief in me fueled this project from its inception. Your encouragement, patience, and understanding throughout the writing process were invaluable. A special thank you to my beta readers, whose insightful feedback helped shape the story into what it is today. Your keen eyes and honest critiques were instrumental in refining the narrative and ensuring a compelling read. Thank you also to my editor, [Editor's Name], for their guidance and expertise. Your insights and suggestions significantly improved the manuscript, and I am incredibly grateful for your dedication and hard work. Finally, thank you to all the readers who have supported my work. Your passion for storytelling is what inspires me to continue writing.

www.ingramcontent.com/pod-product-compliance
Lightning Source LLC
Chambersburg PA
CBHW020021030726
47499CB00007B/2206